Conduit

ALSO BY C.M. BANSCHBACH

The Dragon Keep Chronicles
Oath of the Outcast
Blood of the Seer

The Drifter Duology
Then Comes A Drifter
A Name Long Buried

Spirits' Valley Duology
Greywolf's Heart
Saber's Pride

Drax Guard: Crew Six
Flashpoint
Faultline
Conduit
Stoneheart
Shrike

Fates Defiant

CONDUIT

DRAX GUARD: CREW SIX #3

C.M. BANSCHBACH

Conduit

ISBN: 979-8-9890651-3-4

Published by Campitor Press

clairembanschbach.com

Cover Design: Emilie Haney @eahcreative

Drax Guard Logo: Morlin Lorenz @thatmoonysky

For those with something heavy in the past, it doesn't mean you can't
have a future.

And for my nieces and nephews who all inspired Bear in some way.

1

Remy

Whoever tries to sell you on cuddles with kids has clearly never had a furnace masquerading as a four-year-old human crawl into their bed in the middle of the night and refuse to leave. My long-sleeve shirt is a little damp from where my son is tucked up against my side. I'd think Blair had magic like mine if I hadn't already tested him.

I've been gone for almost two weeks on the last scouting mission with my Drax Guard squad, and from the way things are stirring on our border with the Yukon over the latest territory disputes, it probably won't be long before we're sent out again.

We got back late three days ago, so I'd left my bag by the front door like I always do to let him know I'm home. I got woken up by a yelling juggernaut who promptly burrowed under my arm and refused to leave, waking me back up every time I dozed off during the itemized recap of his last few weeks. Blair's been glued to my side and has invaded every night since.

I've missed him too.

My arm tucks behind my head and I stare at the ceiling, barely visible in the greying light of early dawn. He'll sleep for another hour and then get up to keep my parents busier than I did growing up.

A bit of restlessness grows in my limbs, and I carefully extricate myself from the blankets without waking him. A half-smile tugs. He'd brought the book I'd been reading to him before he fell asleep in his room. I slide it out from the blankets, straighten the bend to the cover, and set it on the nightstand.

He's too young for books about talking animals with weapons, but they were some of my favorites growing up all over the Allied States and for short periods in my parents' native Hawaii. We slowly pick our way through one each time I'm home on leave.

My bare feet slide across the worn floorboards, and I tap the door-frame, checking the warding I always have up. Ever since...

A shudder crawls its way down my spine. Almost five years and I can't shake the feelings left behind by *her*. And sometimes looking at Blair and the way he grins in a coy mischief to try to get his own way will wake the same nausea. But it's not his fault.

And to drive that point home to my doubtful brain, I tuck the blankets up around Blair before I leave the room.

My parents aren't up yet. Yeah, twenty-seven years old and I still live with my parents. Mostly because I made some mistakes, got dumped with a newborn four years ago, and don't trust anyone else to look after my son while I'm away.

The spec ops Drax Guard is different from my first few years in the Army. There's no routinely scheduled leaves and trainings. It's "go" at whatever time and for however long it takes to get the job done. I've been gone anywhere from forty-eight hours to over eight months at a time.

The kitchen is quiet, nothing stirring yet. I get the kettle going. On missions I'll drink the crappy ration pack coffee, because somehow the tea is even worse. At home, my parents and I keep the cabinet well stocked.

I pull down a mug and drop in a bag of Mom's favorite Britannic tea. The kettle slowly warms, and I cross my arms across my chest, staring out the kitchen windows to the front yard as I wait. Hanging plants frame all the windows, and the front gardens are basically jungles. That's the way it's always been in whatever house, in whatever state. My parents are some of the top botanists in the Allied States, hence moving around for different teaching positions my entire life. They're semi-retired now, but the house will always be bursting with flora.

I'm the oddball in the family with zero interest in plants, instead using my inherited wildfire magic for the military. Something my dad disagrees with even if he has the exact same magic that he passed to me. Though sometimes I'm not sure if it's that I'm in the Armed Forces or that I'm not serving in the Hawaiian forces instead. I technically have dual citizenship and could enlist in their Navy, but I'm only three-quarters Island, and never felt like I truly belonged there for one reason or anoth-er.

The clock on the living room mantelpiece softly chimes the hour and I turn to breakfast. We spent a year in the Eastern Allied state of New Jersey and my parents developed a taste for bagels. Toasted to a crisp and served with butter instead of cream cheese. I have no idea how or why, and I refuse any time they destroy one.

And there's also Blair. I do most of the cooking when I'm home. Maybe the closest I get to being a normal dad. The single one who lives with his parents who took him and his kid in without question when he showed up with a surprise baby and no good explanation.

He's four and will eat anything, but he's also got a fondness for waffles. Mostly because they can hold all the syrup he wants. He and Cieran bonded over that the last time my crew sergeant was over.

I start grabbing ingredients from the cabinets while the kettle whistles. They have terrible taste in breakfast, but my parents taught me how to cook. I have a lot of good memories of all three of us in the kitchen, whipping up meals or baked goods from scratch. One of my favorite memories is the two months when I was sixteen when we did a culinary tour of the seven continents and their differing cultures.

Tea steeps while I get everything mixed and the waffle iron heating. I'm pouring the first round in when a, "Waffles!" announces a battering-ram to my leg. My knee crashes into the cabinet, but I can't help but grin back at the sparkling smile turned up at me.

"Hey, Bear."

He's got my thick dark hair and eyes, but his skin tone is a shade or two lighter than my deep brown. He's also got a slimmer build, and likely won't grow into the broad shoulders and more stocky build of me and his grandfather.

"When are they ready?"

"Hold your horses. I don't get a 'good morning' first?"

Blair squeezes around my waist, face straining, before he belts out a "Good morning, Dad!" that's got to have the neighbors stirring. He darts to the fridge, grabs the milk carton and hands it to me. I tip a decent amount into my tea. Blair returns it and holds up his arms for me to sweep him up onto the counter.

"What are we doing today?" I ask.

"We can go to the park. Please!"

"The one with the tall slides?"

His face lights up, and I will probably regret raising a daredevil once we get out there and I see him on top of the thirty-foot slide, but I'm not saying no right now.

The distinctive sound of my mom clearing her throat sounds, and she gets another bellowed greeting from her grandson and a softer version from me. She accepts the waffle Blair brings her, and still raises an eyebrow at me. I give the same look back and she relents slightly as she makes her own tea.

They didn't ask to be practically raising a grandson, and I know how lucky I am that they are. That they haven't given up on me.

Bear scarfs down a waffle and darts off to change from his shark pajamas. Apparently, we are going to the park immediately.

Mom sips at her tea, and I ignore the look she's giving me, spinning my mostly empty mug between my hands.

"Everything okay today, Rem?"

The magic in my veins is jittery, which means nothing good is on the horizon. Memories are popping up without permission this morning. They have been for six months since I saw fae magic coming right at me on a mission, which is leaving a clammy sort of feeling along my forearms where my sleeves are tucked up.

"Yeah."

Her lips purse and her hand presses to my arm. "What's going on?"

"Just normal off-duty brooding." I try to smile, but she's not buying it. "I'll be okay."

"Do you know how long this time before you're off again?" I know she tries to keep the faint bitterness from her tone. Fed by the worry that comes from having your only child sign on with the military at nineteen and then work his way up to the elite Drax Guard and be given some of the most dangerous jobs.

"I don't." Sometimes it's weeks, sometimes months, sometimes days or hours, before we're called up again. "But I'm gonna try to spend enough time with him."

Mom shakes her head a little but thankfully doesn't veer toward an old argument that I'd have more time to spend with my son if I took a discharge. Found somewhere else to use the magic whirling through me. That there's never "enough" time to spend with a growing child.

But the only place I want to be is armored up with sword on my hip and basalt-inlaid short sword on my back, magic ready to spring from my hands, looking out for my team.

She pats my arm, the "tell me when you change your mind" clear in her little sigh. "I'll clean up," she says.

My fingers press against my mug. A faint hiss between my teeth has the last of the tea boiling in a second, steam bursting. But the release of magic doesn't still the twisting inside. I wave a hand over the top of the mug, quieting the intensity, and shove back to dump the mug in the sink.

But when I take the five steps from the kitchen into the living area, Blair is camped at the small table, papers and colors everywhere. His shirt is on backwards. Hopefully he got the pants right. Light catches his eyes when he looks up at me, and I can only see *her* and a hint of purple in their dark depths. I jolt and he's just his energetic self, brows pinched quizzically.

He doesn't even have the pointed fae ears like he should. Fae genetics usually override human when they pair up, leaving pointed ears and a band of either vibrant grey or purple around the iris. But he looks just as human as me except for the little hints of her here and there.

I shrug my shoulders, trying to get rid of the unease, and clear my throat. "What are you working on?"

Blair holds some residual caution from my reaction, and guilt trickles in to mix with the unease. It's not his fault someone messed my head up.

"I didn't finish my pictures last night," he says.

I ease onto the couch, leaning forward on my knees. "Can I see?"

Blair pushes a few papers toward me. One swivels under my fingers.

"It's from our book." He doesn't look up, face concentrating as he colors. It's a recognizable mouse holding an overlarge sword.

"That's pretty good, Bear."

He beams, and it's catching glimpses of his grandparents in the sparkling eyes and dimples. "I'm making you now." He lifts a color-streaked hand and turns the paper for me to see for a second before resuming.

My head's a little too big and one arm is really jacked, but he's four.

"Can I see your tattoo? I want to make it right." He barely looks up. The giant arm is the one tattooed in real life. It pricks at me again, but I can't really ever say no to him. And no one is going to see this except the house.

I tug up the left sleeve of my shirt as far as I can. I've been wearing long-sleeves for five years, not always around the Guard, but definitely out in public. My warlock tattoo is three broad bands around my forearm. The middle one holds inverted triangles around a thick line—wild magic. The bottom band has spirals through a solid band. Fire. And the top is just a set of three slender lines to make things look more even.

"I want to make the dragon too."

I shake my head and try to get the sleeve up a little higher. A magma dragon curls up my upper arm, its tail dipping below the top bands and twining around them. The elf tattoo artist did a really good job back when I was a little more cocky about my magic and skill. But I'm going to have to take the shirt off for him to see the full thing, and I'm not doing that.

He sighs a little, but starts drawing, casting glances at my arm.

"Dad..." It's said cautiously, and the speed of his drawing slows. I'm about to get hit by a *question*.

"Yeah?" I'm bracing myself for something like he stole cookies last night or what happens to plants when they die.

"How come I don't have a mom?"

It punches my gut.

"The other kids at the park have moms, but I only have you. And Grandma says she's *your* mom." The look he gives me squeezes my heart, making me almost nauseous. There's a soft clatter behind me, but I don't dare look at Mom.

I'm scrambling, trying to find something that won't make me explode in bitterness. "Because you showed up as an egg one night and I had to keep you wrapped up in a towel until you hatched."

His "I know you're *lying*," look is followed by laughter.

"Go get ready to go to the park. It'll be too hot later."

He obeys, hopping to his feet and sending some markers flying. I pick them up, capping a few, and turn slowly at the gentle clearing of a throat.

Mom stands behind the couch, cupping a light blue mug in her hands. "When are you going to tell him?" she asks softly.

I jam a lid on savagely. "Maybe when I can stomach thinking about it."

"Rem..." She just thinks my ex dumped the both of us. She's never going to know the truth either.

"I'm going to change. We'll be back before lunch." I leave the room before she can ask some other probing question. Besim does a good job of being team mom, asking the deep questions you'd rather not answer, or giving the pursed lip look to hide amusement or weary *doneness* with shenanigans. But an actual mom is still scarier.

She doesn't say anything to me as we leave, but gives Blair a hug and reminder to be good. We have to stop for a second to get his shoes on the correct feet, and I tap his Army ballcap down over his eyes before we get out the door. He pushes it up indignantly and claims my hand.

Our three-block walk to the park is slowed by investigating the bug crawling across the sidewalk, waving at the ancient dog who always comes to meet passers-by at its gate, picking up sticks and a "really cool rock."

It's already starting to get warm; summers in central Oregon always are. Sunlight hits off Dunhare's sidewalks and buildings, and vehicles' power crystals give off some extra heat as they're rigged to pull power from sunlight to last longer. People are out and about in the parks, soaking up the sun before winter comes back around in a few months to bury us in grey and sleet and rain.

I always get a few looks for wearing long-sleeves. Even the lightweight, breathable fabric is not really practical. Especially for a fire warlock like me whose internal temperature runs higher than normal humans. On days like these, I'll tuck the sleeves up just high enough to keep the tattoos covered.

Blair's in short sleeves, but he's started wanting to wear jeans and boots like I do. I've caught him drawing on his left arm at least once. It makes me feel very inadequate. Maybe a better dad wouldn't, but I've kind of felt like I'm struggling along, making it up as I go, for the last four years.

We come around the corner and Blair runs ahead to the slides with my permission. I meander after him. A few other kids scramble around, so he'll be content enough for now. I find a bench and sink down, half-heartedly returning the waves from the moms sitting or walking around with strollers.

They know I'm military and some are annoyingly forward, sometimes coming over and pestering with updates about Blair, or hinting questions about my love life—or lack thereof—that are about a subtle as a wild-magic grenade.

Guess my face is uninviting enough today. They stay on their side of the park and I keep on mine, acknowledging my daredevil son with waves and letting him know I am, in fact, watching. Once or twice my heart rises in my throat as he starts climbing somewhere high. My hand cups, ready to throw out a catching spell if I can't sprint there in time. And his "I got it!" is not remotely reassuring.

But he makes it every time, and I sink back onto the bench. He's on top of the tallest slide, ready to come down, when his gaze slides past me and lights up again.

"Cieran! Watch!"

I twist to see my sergeant coming up to the bench, hands in his jeans pockets, the glint of his prosthetic leg through the hole in the right knee.

"Let's see it, Bear!" he calls back. His ballcap is on backwards as usual. It's faded and battered, but it's still holding the *staying* charm from the fae on his old team who were lost on a mission gone bad almost two years ago. I've offered to do the same to something newer whenever he's ready, but he hasn't taken me up on it.

"Hey." I sit back.

"Rem." He stands next to me, his feet braced wider and hands still in jeans pockets. "Swung by the house and they said you'd be over here."

Readiness settles in my gut. There's really only one reason he'd be here. I'd hoped for a little more time between missions, but this is the way it goes sometimes. "What is it this time?"

"Not sure." The reply destroys the certainty. "Got a call from the CO a bit ago. He wants the two of us in his office. Asked for you by name."

"For what?" I'm halfway up. Embers of magic start stirring again as the same unease from earlier flares.

Cieran shrugs. "Was wondering if you knew anything."

But I'm feeling clueless. There's been nothing from the last few missions, and things have been quiet on leave. Blair scampers over, racing to Cieran who bends down to catch and heave him into the air with flailing limbs and laughter.

Blair had seemed happy enough to get a new "uncle." Cieran's been running Crew Six for the last six months as our new sergeant. He's getting his feet back under him after losing his old crew to a mission, and then his sister to cancer. Right after which he got sent back out to the very place he lost his team, faced down their murderer, and got carted back on a stretcher again. Standard mission stuff.

"Hey, hooligan." Cieran switches Blair's cap backwards.

"Dad said I hatched from an egg."

Cieran doesn't miss a beat, nodding seriously. "Yeah, I heard about that. Bright pink and sparkly, right?"

"No!" Blair howls and slings arms around Cieran's neck as he laughs. Cieran half-throws him around so Blair's on his back instead. He's taken Bear in stride, but he's got a few other "nieces" and "nephews" from the families of former Crew Eight.

"I don't want to go yet!" Blair protests as Cieran and I turn toward the park entrance.

"Sorry, kiddo. Your dad and I have to go talk about some work stuff." Cieran carries him as we head back for the sidewalk.

Blair quiets, focusing on me. "Will you have to leave again?"

Cieran and I share a wordless look. There's no place we'd rather be, but maybe sometimes it's a little too easy to leave family behind.

"Not sure yet, Bear. I'll be back in a bit."

He takes my reassurance, and steals Cieran's hat so it doesn't poke him in the face. We make it back a lot faster with Blair contained, and he tries to bargain his way to coming to the command tower with us. Finally, Mom gets him distracted by a snack, and we leave.

We opt to walk, and it's fifteen minutes at a brisk pace to the Allied States Army base that takes up the northwest quadrant of Dunhare.

"What did you do this morning to piss your mom off?" Cieran asks.

I shove hands in my pockets again. It's a little weird having Cieran as our sergeant. I'd only known him before as a different crew's officer and he was never one to really act on rank. His old crew was full of pranks, but serious about jobs. He's two years older than me, which also makes it weird. Our old sergeant Pothos was just over forty when he went reserves nine months ago.

"Just stuff with Bear," I reply shortly, not wanting to get into it. Even our crew doesn't know the full story and I've been with Besim and Dejan for almost five years.

"Ah." He nods. "It's not easy in your position. I watched Javi and Masood struggle with it too."

At least his old crewmates had wives who were still there for the kids.

"I know you're doing the best you can."

It's a little bit of a balm to go with the stab. "Yeah, well, a lot of the time it doesn't seem that way. There's just..." But I'm not about to tell him. "Just some crap I'm trying to figure out."

"Okay," he says easily. "If you need to talk through anything, let me know."

I nod, but not sure I'll ever take him up on it. Maybe after we've served for another fifteen years and probably not even then.

"Why didn't you just call?" I ask instead.

He shrugs. "Was already out stretching my legs. Easier to swing by."

Out walking to make himself tired enough to sleep later. Or trying to get rid of some memories by walking faster.

"You doing okay, Sarge?" I ask. That's easier than talking about me.

He scrubs a hand across the back of his neck. "Yeah. Coming up on the date."

The day he and his team were ambushed in the Wastelands, and he was the only one who made it home outside a body bag.

"You need anything?"

"A memory wipe isn't going to do much good in the long run." Cieran's smile is a little pained. "Families want me to do dinner on the day, but..." He trails off, shoulders slumping.

I search for something. "I'll make pie for you to take, just give me the credit for it."

A smile touches his lips. "Maybe I'll just eat it at home myself on the kitchen floor."

We make it through the base security checkpoint with a quick inspection of ID's. There's an easy way to get his mind off things. "Heard from Athina recently?"

He brightens like a kid on Christmas Day at the mention of the dragon shifter he's heartbonded to, also courtesy of the Wastelands mission eight months ago. A lot happened.

"Yeah, she and the fleet will be here in a few days for another joint training."

He's in the Allied States Drax Guard, she's part of a different country's military force from thousands of miles away. They've only seen each other a few times in person since the heartbond activated, though their mental link keeps them connected. Part of the arrangement for them both staying active duty is wearing heartbond dampeners when they're on missions for security reasons. But he doesn't have the copper-inlaid bracelet on his left wrist, so all's good for now.

The shadow of the command tower falls across our path, killing any follow-up question. The jittering unease is back, and I just want to get this over with as quick as possible.

2

REMY

"You sure you have no idea what this is?" Cieran asks.

I shake my head. He's just as uneasy as me. No soldier likes walking into the unknown, and a summons to command without the whole crew reeks of something unpleasant.

Silence stays between us as we jog the stairs up into the tower, striding across the atrium's mosaiced floor displaying our insignia—a bloody fire drake coiled around a sword. The reason for the Guard's founding, front and center. Dunhare was once a nowhere Army camp over two hundred years ago when a civil war was tearing the states apart. Then came a fire drake invasion and that created alliances real fast.

Four of the best soldiers, both indigenous and immigrant, teamed up to strike at the volcanic nest. But the combination of magic in the air and soil from natural reservoirs and years of fighting sparked an eruption that turned the nest into a supervolcano and wiped out half the states. The damage turned the fledgling country into the Allied States of America and left the Wastelands as a scar across the map. Our flag reflects it—two fields of blue separated just off-center with three alternating stripes of red and white, and stars for the remaining states dot the eastern and western halves.

A mural of the four men resides above the wall of honor—rows upon rows of soldiers over the last two hundred years who followed in their footsteps and didn't make it back. Cieran's old crew is up there, but he barely spares it a glance. I wouldn't want to pause and look at the dead faces of brothers every time I walked through the door either.

We take the elevator up to the fourth floor. The dwarf mechanics have finally fixed the pulley system and it doesn't feel like cheating death stepping into the damn thing.

CO's office is at the end of the hall and the door is open. Cieran and I give each other one more look and stride in. He's first, and it takes me an extra second to nerve myself up, palms clammy in a way they haven't been since before my testing into the Guard.

"Sergeant." CO's voice sets the tone. We've got civilians or other officers inside. I'm wishing for the comfort of my armor and swords as I step in.

Captain Bron Wolfe stands behind his desk. He's in the dark grey fatigues of the Guard, with rank bars on his right lapel. Cieran's at attention, hands behind his back, and there's two women standing to the left of the desk. Wolfe's aide stands in the corner opposite. Eckhart's a mountain cougar shifter and always seems poised for action. It's not helping me relax.

"Specialist." Wolfe greets me.

"Sir." I salute and brace myself under the stares of the women.

"This is Sergeant Cieran O'Donnell and Specialist Remy Kalama." Wolfe waves to us, and then indicates the women. "Agents Ariane Fortin—" He points to the older of the two women, short hair and wiry frame. Human from the looks of her, but I'm picking up the low-level hum of magic that alerts warlocks to each other.

"And Sara Alder." He points to the younger holding a folder and, more interestingly, a knife strapped to her thigh. Though the way she stands makes it seem she's trying to get away from it. Her reddish-blonde hair is pulled back to reveal pointed ears, though lacking the sharpness of a full elf or fae. Definitely doesn't have the band of vibrant grey or purple around the iris that marks half-fae. As she moves, the light glints off only hints of silver in her green eyes. Half-elf.

"Agents," Cieran greets them, and I tip a nod.

Wolfe heaves a breath. "Specialist, close the door, and let's all have seats."

Yeah, this is hella reassuring.

I tug at my left shirtsleeve as I sit down. Extra chairs have been brought in and face each other in sets of two with Wolfe's desk completing a lopsided U shape. At least Cieran's knee bobs just as much as mine.

"We're with the Bureau of Magical Affairs," Fortin starts and Cieran and I exchange a glance. The BMA and the Drax Guard don't have a great track record with each other, managing mostly to get crossways with each other on any case overlap.

"It's not what you think," she hastens, and we then look immediately to Wolfe, who sits back in his chair, arm propped on the rest and chin in hand. He inclines his head slightly. *Hear her out.*

Fortin gets our attention. She's noticed the silent exchange and is maybe a little pissed by it, but neither of us apologize. Alder sits silently, hands clenched around the folder, knees jiggling like ours.

"We've been tracking a fae. She'd dipped off our lists a few years ago, but recently popped back up. Maeve Ballagh."

My flinch is picked up by everyone in the room.

"And that's why you're here, Specialist."

All the unease drains from my limbs, rushing to pool in my gut like a hundred-pound boulder.

"You had a run-in with her almost five years ago, I believe?"

The way she's "asking," she already knows.

"Yes, ma'am." I barely get it out, back pressing harder against the chair.

"That doesn't seem to be the general reaction to her," Fortin says drily. "Alder?"

The younger edges forward, cracking open the folder and extending a piece of paper to me. I have to force my hand to take it.

"She came up in response to some anti-trafficking raids over the last few months. Someone's been after kids, mostly with magic, any species." Alder's got a clear voice, but it's laden with something else. Something regarding the paper I'm still not looking at.

"This was found at a house raided three days ago. Those we detained listed her as an accomplice in shuffling a few elf and fae kids over the Vinland border recently. She'd been lying low at that house for a while. They said she'd been interested in some of the kids and testing them somehow. She left some stuff behind when the team went in. Uh..." She gestures to me.

I finally look down, but Cieran beats me to it by the faint inhale on my left. It's a copy of a notebook page, fluid writing listing out four names. Three are crossed off, and mine's the only one left untouched at the bottom.

"What the hell?" Cieran mutters.

Shit. My eyes shut for a moment, and when I open them, I'm staring back at the two agents. Cieran leans forward trying to get a better look at my face.

"What's the thought?" I manage.

"We've tracked down the other three names, all men as you can see." Alder speaks again and I'm trying to focus, but my mind slips dangerously back to five years ago, my shoulders already curling under the weight of it all.

"They seem to remember seeing her recently, but have no clear memory of how or where. We've picked up no sightings, and all scans and surveillance feeds have been negative in the city and surrounding areas. So that leaves you." The apology is clear in her voice and the way she leans toward me, but I'm already pulling back.

"Don't worry. I know enough to run the other way when I see her," I try to say lightly but it comes out a strangled mess. Run like I should have years ago.

"Any reason she might be coming around?" Fortin doesn't beat around the bush. Normally I'd appreciate it, but right now I'd rather be anywhere else.

"She made it pretty clear we were parting ways five years ago," I say. Heat tingles in my palms and I clench my fists to stop magic from sparking. Cieran's knee nudges mine, but it's not enough. I need *out*.

The agents exchange a glance this time.

Alder leans forward again. "If she hasn't been in contact with you yet, there's a good chance she will be. And you might be our best bet to catching her. We think we can link her to a bunch of other nasty stuff."

"Good luck with that." A sardonic smile flashes across my face. Maeve was good at covering her tracks. I guess I should also be surprised she gave me her real name all those years ago. But full fae don't normally tend to lie, still restricted a little by a few of the old rules from before the Courts were broken.

"We've got evidence for a few things." Fortin takes over. "We'd like your cooperation, Specialist. You'd be working with one of our teams, and we'll be calling in local—"

"No." Cieran leaves little room for argument. "If he's in, you're getting Crew Six as your team and his backup."

Wolfe arches an eyebrow and Cieran just stares back. But it seems the CO is already on the same track.

"We don't leave our people behind, Agents," Wolfe says. "There's precedent here for a Drax Guard crew teaming up with the Agency."

The agents look us over. I'd be a hell of a lot more comfortable with my crew behind me, instead of this agent who sits like the knife on her thigh is stabbing her. If the rest of their team is like that, we're screwed.

"Okay." Fortin nods. "You guys have a reputation, but I'm hoping for full cooperation."

Cieran gives a quick laugh. "Right back at you, Agent."

She takes it with a slight tip of the head. "Okay then. Specialist, you have any family? We'll put a team with them just to make sure."

"My parents." My throat goes dry again. "And my son."

Alder smooths her hands over the folder like it might be hiding something else.

"I'm going to ask this bluntly, Specialist," Fortin says. "Is Ballagh the mother?"

I mutely nod, and I can feel Cieran's sharp regard fall to me.

"Any wife, girlfriend...ex...she might be willing to go after for leverage if needed?" Fortin at least sounds concerned.

"No, ma'am." I force myself to keep her gaze.

"All right. Why don't you let them know what will be happening and that they'll have some company for a few days. Sergeant, get your crew together. We'll have a briefing at twelve hundred hours?" She checks with everyone in the room. That's barely two hours from now. More than enough time.

Fortin turns to Wolfe as we all stand, and Cir and I escape, reading the request for a private follow-up conversation loud and clear. I half-expect Cieran to linger outside the door, but he strides down the hall. I follow until he turns into a smaller briefing room and shoves the door open.

His look spears right through me. "Inside."

My palms sting again as I obey, magic desperate to come out and protect from the invisible threat.

Cieran shuts the door behind us. "What the hell is going on, Rem?"

He's going to have to wait a second, because I'm about to be sick. Except it never comes, and nausea just rocks through me in endless waves. I sink back against the wall, slipping down to a crouch, head hanging low.

"Remy?" He's closer, tone gentler, but I still don't dare to look up. "I need to know what we're walking into here."

He wants to give me time, space, I can read it in the way he keeps back a few paces, but he's also right and the team deserves to know.

I scrape a hand down my face and manage to get standing again. It's just concern on his face when I meet his look, but it's about to vanish along with all respect for me. I look around the room, almost desperate, but nothing is going to help me. I lift my hand, fingers tucked together, and then twist, spreading a well of silence over us and the room. Anything I say will be contained in this room.

Cieran tilts his head, but he doesn't argue.

"Uh…" It's barely enough to steady my voice. "I met…her…almost five years ago. Had just got my pin, was on top of the world."

There's a faint smile. He remembers what it was like to get the Drax pin.

"Young and stupid." My scuffing feet draw my attention. "We went out a few times. She knew how to party, but we never did anything more than that. Maybe because I knew in the back of my mind something was off about her." Maybe that made it worse, I hadn't ever quite decided.

"Until one night, about four months in to seeing each other, she came over, bottle of whiskey in hand. I don't know what was in it, but it went straight to my head. I'd been smart enough to keep a few warding charms up against her glamour, but they slipped that night, or..." I shake my head. The next words stick but Cieran waits patiently.

I choke out a sound, maybe a laugh, maybe a sob. "I think a case could be made for dubious consent on my end because I..." My face is red-hot, every bit of me on fire with shame. "I don't remember most of it. When I woke up in the morning, she was gone and I felt drugged. Magic, alcohol, something else...maybe all three." I shrug.

"Shit, Rem."

I still can't look at him, not wanting to see the look. But it's all spilling out now, not content until I've gotten through all of it.

"She disappeared. Not a word, until ten months later when she showed up at my door with a newborn."

A sound I'm afraid to interpret breaks from him.

"Said she didn't want him, that he wasn't what she *needed*. She took off, and I haven't seen her since."

My arms tuck across my chest, palms pressing to my sides, trying to keep myself together. A brush against my shoulder has me tipping a slight look.

Cieran leans against the wall beside me. "If Bear didn't look enough like you, I'd be asking…"

"I tested him that night. He's mine." I put some more space between us, afraid to take the sign that he might not be disgusted with me and my mistake.

"Shit." He shakes his head. "Anyone else know what happened?"

"Pothos knew some. He caught me on a day when I was…not doing so good." My old sergeant had stopped me from doing anything too stupid, helped me get my head on a little straighter.

"Hey." His hand on my shoulder brings my focus up reluctantly. Seriousness lines his face, and under it is concern as he checks me over. "That's some heavy stuff that you didn't have to tell me. We barely know each other. But I'm glad you did."

I still can't really look at him.

"You guys were telling me this plenty eight months ago, so now it's your turn to hear it. We've got your back here, Rem."

A different sort of feeling pushes up through the shame. Not quite relief. But, "I messed up," my hushed voice falls between us. "I made a mistake, I…"

"Hey." He shakes me a little. "From what you said, you were still playing it smart. Sounds like it was all her. Full fae have powerful magic, Rem. Takes a lot to stand against them."

"But I should have known." My head shakes. "I should have…"

"Remy." He barely stills the tremors rocking through me. "I know you've seen some of the ugly in this world. And sometimes that shit gets us too. I've only got pieces, but it sounds like she might have been targeting you. And she was going to do whatever it took to get her way. None of that is your fault."

But I'm still shaking, trying to get away from those words.

I didn't do enough. And now I'm risking family because she might be back for something. Another blow comes. *"...interested in some of the kids and testing them somehow."* Might be back for Blair.

I fold forward under the weight of the realization, but Cieran's got me.

"What if she's coming for Blair?"

His eyes harden at my fearful admission. "Then we take her out."

I jerk a nod. That's the first thing to really break through.

"Hey." Cieran's voice drops again, and he still has hold of my shoulders. "Some of this might come out, but it's not going to change anything between you and the crew. Okay?" His gentle shake orders my burning face up. "Not between us." He flicks a hand from me to him. "And I know Dejan and Besim will say the same."

Dejan would just start filling his quiver and Besim sharpening his longsword. They were ready to go when I fed them the partial truth that an old girlfriend had dumped our kid on me, and we barely knew each other then.

"Yeah." I manage a nod.

Cieran sort of looks up at me, checking me over, making sure I'm not going to fall apart. He'd know the signs, and suddenly I'm glad it's him who knows. He knows what it's like to have guilt pressing down, intent on dogging steps. Maybe I can ask him sometime how he's gotten rid of his.

"This stays between us until you say different, okay?" he says.

I clear my throat, trying to nod again.

"You just tell us what you need out there." Cieran's fist taps my shoulder. "You're not alone in this."

"You're right." I sniff and back away. "Hearing that is really annoying."

He chuckles. "Payback's a *crytch*." But he gets another fistbump to my arm and I get myself together, pulling down the silencing spell.

"Gear?" he asks.

"Most is at home."

"Okay. Head there, make sure things are set at your place. I'll get my stuff and have the guys meet us for the briefing."

I nod and he turns to open the door.

"Hey, Sarge?"

He tilts a look back.

"Thanks." I halfheartedly lift a hand.

"You're welcome. And, Rem? I'm serious. It's not your fault."

He disappears, leaving me with the confusing feeling in my chest. It's almost like relief.

3

Sara

I hate awkward conversations. Which probably means I'm in the wrong profession. Agent analyst at the BMA, and the recent work with the trafficking division to help them sort patterns and data has led to some interesting situations.

But the just-finished meeting might have been one of the worst in a while. The three other guys on the list had been a little embarrassed they'd been played by a fae, and a little eager to find out anything about her whereabouts no matter that she was involved in trafficking. But there was definitely something else to Specialist Kalama's encounters with her.

He's listed as a fire warlock—human with innate elemental based magic—but no marks visible because he's somehow in long sleeves in the middle of summer. And it's promising to be a muggy day.

But the three other men—an elf, a human warlock with two degrees making him a wizard with a superiority complex, and a half-fae—all had magic of some sort as well. And the other linking factor is…they all have kids with Maeve.

Fortin dismisses me a few minutes after the soldiers leave. She and the commander are going over logistics. Maybe I can finally go get lunch. I skipped breakfast except for a hurried glass of orange juice, and that's long gone.

I exit into the hall. The thing I like about this building is it's straight-forward, no twists and turns, or hidden corridors, or storage closets masquerading as offices. Soldiers like things simple, and that gives my brain an easier time figuring out where to go while focusing on a million other things.

The folder rotates in my hands as I wait for the elevator, fingers tapping on the smooth surface to the beat of the song that's been stuck in my head for the last three days. The click of a door hits pause for a second.

Specialist Kalama comes out of a room and his shoulders are slumped. I quickly look away and wait until his even tread halts beside me at the elevator doors to look up and flash a small smile.

His returning smile is just sort of the turned-up corner of the mouth people give when they're trying to be polite and don't want to engage. Or to fill up the awkward space that's waiting for an elevator or a bus or standing in line at a coffee shop.

"Hey." I half-turn and he jolts a little. "Um...I just wanted to say sorry for dumping all this on you. I'm sure this is not what you wanted to hear this morning. Or any morning."

Kalama gives a wan sort of smile. "What, hearing the ex from hell is back and might be coming to pull you into some other shit?" He winces faintly. "Sorry."

I wave the apology for the curse away. "I've heard worse, believe me, Specialist..." I catch myself. "Sir?"

This time there's a faint laugh. "You can just call me Remy. Specialist isn't an important enough rank to get technical."

I nod and we step into the elevator as it swishes open. We take opposite corners and he sticks hands in his pockets. And my attempt to make it not awkward has just kept it awkward. I shift the folder up against my chest, fingers starting to tap again. We both watch the lights tick down the floor numbers.

"Is there any good place to eat around here?" My sudden question has him jolting again, shocking him out of whatever deep thought had him gnawing on the inside of his lip. Not that I was watching in the blurry reflection of the doors.

"Uh...diner around the corner is pretty awful, so go for the food truck a block west. Pakistani elf couple runs it, and they make some killer wraps."

My stomach growls and I cover it up with an appreciative noise.

"The regular wrap has a good kick, so don't get spicy unless you like getting your mouth melted." A more real half-smile flickers.

"Good to know." I nod. "Thanks."

The elevator dings and he holds back to let me go first.

"I guess I'll see you in a bit." I offer a slight wave.

"Yeah, see you later."

And that look returns. Somewhere between fear and *sick*. I offer a smile because there's not much more I can do. A protection detail will already be heading over to his house, and the briefing in a few hours will probably just make everything feel worse with additional information.

Sometimes, I really hate my job.

I beat him outside and definitely pretend to be checking something on my tablet when I hear another masculine voice call, "Rem!"

A figure with a slighter build compared to the Specialist's stockier shoulders jogs up. They pause together and I'm *not* eavesdropping. We didn't get much of anything on the other members of his squad other than names and ranks. The Drax Guard keeps things locked up tight when it comes to their squads and identities. My half-elf hearing is pretty good but still can't pick up anything specific, almost like one of them might be throwing up a small charm or ward to mask conversation.

I'm nosy and sneak a glance. And get hit by a stony look from the newcomer's bright silver-green eyes. Full elf, and there's something lethal about him, until Remy taps his arm and makes a pleading motion with his hand. The elf backs down slightly, still scowling at me. But it doesn't seem like the sort of judgment I sometimes get from full elves for being only half myself. He backs away and Remy accompanies him with a glance back over his shoulder.

Wonderful. Fortin and I had already been grumbling about working with local Dunhare police, but teaming up with the Drax Guard might be even more prickly and difficult to navigate. And I don't even need to be a good analyst to figure that out. All I need are stories from the Bureau, obviously embellished to make our agents look good, and the clincher—the quick interaction and the way Remy and his sergeant had been looking at us in the briefing.

Can't wait to see how this goes.

4

REMY

DEJAN STICKS TO MY side on the walk home. He's scowling, but that's sort of his usual look most days. Like every other sane person around, he wears short sleeves, and there's a knife hidden where his jeans are tucked into half-laced boots. He'd probably be carrying his carbon fiber bow if it wasn't so conspicuous. His magic, even though tuned for healing with the typical elf *regeneration* and *nurture*, can still pack a pretty good kick if he needs.

He's full elf, which means he's just barely shorter than the average human, and therefore the shortest on our team. I've barely got him beat, standing just at six feet on a good day. But he's also the oldest, and I fried apple fritters for his forty-fifth this year. But again, elf with a two-hundred-year life expectancy, so forty-five in elf years is actually somewhere in the late twenties per human standards. There's a math problem that can figure it out.

"You sure they can help?" Dejan still glares. After I managed a reassurance that Agent Alder wasn't the one to blame entirely for the news, he'd backed off slightly and declared he was coming with me. I'm not sure what Cieran told him and Besim, but Dej must have already been at the command tower for how fast he'd tracked me down. Even if he wasn't, it's not that far from where he lives on base.

"I don't know," I admit, everything else sticking inside. I gave him the bare report—that my ex is after me and maybe Bear. I don't know how to say anything else.

We've been close for almost five years even if we didn't get along during Hell Week. He's prickly to people he doesn't know on a good day, doesn't talk a lot about his past other than the last fifteen years he's spent in Dunhare or nearby Portland as a paramedic before the enlisted forces and eventually Drax Guard.

Everything is ramped up in the week where you make or break to test into the Guard. And even after that, we were constantly at each other's throats once assigned to the same crew. Until I barely saved the both of us from a magic blast he might have accidentally set off, then punched him for being so reckless. He responded by wordlessly slapping a healing spell on my dislocated shoulder. And everything settled between us.

I still feel bad for putting Besim through all that. He has the patience of a saint.

I rely on both of them, many days feeling closer to them than my own family because Besim and Dejan have lived through all the same things as I have these last years. All except for Maeve Ballagh, and I don't know if I can stand for them to know the whole truth and see what might change between us.

"You good, Rem?" he asks, light bootsteps briefly pausing. I check my pace to not leave him behind, but don't look at him.

"Yeah."

His scoff announces the elf word he doesn't say. *Ancrit.* Yeah, I wouldn't believe me either.

A magpie lands in our path, ruffling feathers and cocking head. Dejan's already scanning, and I'm keeping an eye on the bird. Magpies are native to Oregon, but they normally don't look right at you like they know you.

Warmth curls in my palm, magic humming in my veins, bringing comfort to counteract the cold whirling in my gut. A purple glint tinges its eye, then it opens its beak.

"Remy." A purring voice sends ice through me and threatens to extinguish the flame flickering in my palm. She's somewhere out there using the bird as a go-between. That's an old fae trick. Since they pull magic directly from the environment, fae and nature are inextricably bound.

"What do you want?" I grit out.

"Oh." The magpie's beak clicks with the sound. "After all the good times we had? That's how you greet me?" It sidles closer until I nudge it back with my boot. Its wings flare, flapping a few beats. "You've been talking to Agents already. They're efficient, I have to give them that."

"What do you want?" I draw out the words.

Dejan hisses a negative behind me. He doesn't have an eye on anything. I snap my fingers then flick them open, releasing the spell as the sparks drop and skitter away. It's a searching spell. A simple one that doesn't need a verbal component.

"Maybe to see our son."

"He's not yours." Anger coils. I'm about to crush this bird.

"I've got some unfortunate stretch marks that say otherwise, Rem."

I hate the way she says my name, drawn out over the *m* even through a magpie beak.

"You want me to cut it off?" Dejan murmurs behind me. I want to nod, if only to silence her voice, but my spell still spins its search, and we need more time.

"Let's just cut to the chase, Remy. I want you again. You can follow my little friend here and we can get this over with. The Bureau doesn't have to get involved. And as much as I'd love to meet your friends, I don't want them around either."

"No." Dejan says it the same time as I do. But he doesn't know what he's saying no to.

The magpie laughs and it's a croaking version of her bell-like laugh that used to have my heart hopping around. My spell's dying out. It can't find anything in a hundred-yard radius.

"Don't make me pull our son into this. What's that charming name you call him? Bear?"

I still. He doesn't go by that outside the family and the crew. Which means she's already been around, watching, and waiting.

The bird cocks its head again. "Think about it, Remy. You have until tonight. You never really saw what I was capable of. I'd hate to have to show you."

It flies away, narrowly dodging a curl of silver-green magic from Dejan. He curses. I take off into a run toward home, trying to outpace the words and the nausea pushing back up.

She's been spying and who knows what else.

The front door smashes open under my rush. Dad jerks around the couch, one hand raised to cast, and body angled like he's going to try to shelter the potted plant he's holding in his other hand. My gaze slips past him to settle on Blair, sitting wide-eyed at the table, marker in hand. Dejan is right behind me. I fold over, hands on knees in utter relief that they're okay for now.

Mom comes around the corner, bowl and batter-covered spoon in hand. "What's going on?"

"Dej," I say.

But he's already closing the door, making sure everything outside is clear. I press a hand to the doorway, making sure the wards are in place, and adding an extra one or five.

Dad clears his throat. He knows my reasons for doing it, but he's always been a professor and doesn't understand the soldier side of me. "You want to start talking, son?"

My hands press against the wood frame, my head bowing. Dejan is right beside me, offering me a slight nod. He still doesn't know the whole truth, but he's there for me.

I can't keep my parents waiting. Mom's a little more patient, but Dad's an Islander through and through, and despite his normal easygoing mood, you don't say no or keep truths from him. Even as an adult.

I slowly turn. "We need to talk. Dej, can you keep an eye on Bear?"

"Sure thing." The elf moves over to my son, who still watches me cautiously.

"All good, Bear. I'll be back in a second." I muster a smile. Dejan barely stops himself from grabbing Blair as he darts over to me and throws arms around my waist.

"Love you, Dad," he mumbles into my shirt.

A curse almost breaks free, but then I'd get a smack from Mom's wooden spoon for cussing in front of the four-year-old. I bend over, kissing the top of his head.

"Love you, too. Hang out with Dejan for a bit, okay?"

"Okay." Blair slowly draws away, backing over to Dejan who drops to a crouch.

"What are we working on over here?" Dej tugs at some of the papers. He's a grumpy, stoic elf, but there's a softie in there somewhere.

I keep glancing back as Mom and Dad lead the way into the kitchen. It's far enough around the corner that Blair probably won't hear but it's not going to stop Dejan with his elvish hearing.

Mom sets the bowl on the counter and leans up against the sink. Dad broadens his stance, beefy arms crossed over his chest. His family tattoos are visible, the ones I inherited for my warlock marks. He doesn't hide his marks the way I have for five years. The way we're positioned feels like I'm fifteen after being caught with a cigarette at school.

Dad softens a little. "What's going on, Remy?"

"You know a little bit about Blair's...mom." They hadn't gotten the full story either, because I couldn't stomach telling them everything after showing up on their doorstep with a month-old kid having to explain that he was mine. Then moving in with them.

My arms squeeze across my chest. I'd intended to take this to my grave, but here I am about to confess it twice in one day. It stumbles from me, and I'm remembering a little more now that I'm letting myself think about it.

Fates, I really hope Bear can't hear or understand any of this. Cause I'm about to break down admitting that I didn't get a say that night. I can't look at them, keeping my focus on the white tile floor, Mom's house shoes and Dad's heavier boots. He must have been out in the back garden, no time to take them off, before I smashed through the door.

"I got a visit from the Bureau today. They've linked her to some trafficking rings. Think she's involved with some other stuff. And just a few minutes ago, she made contact...threatened Bear unless...I don't know exactly what she wants, and...she just...*used* me..." My hands shake even pinned to my sides under my arms.

There's a smell of magic in the kitchen, crisp and sharp like midnight wildfires, and I don't dare look up to see Dad's enraged face as he tries to suppress the magic boiling up in his veins. Might be a mild-mannered research-professor most of the time, but he passed the fiery magic of the Islands to me.

Mom's hand rubs my upper arm, and then she hugs me. I've got Dad's height, and she barely comes up to my shoulder anymore.

"Why didn't you tell us?" she murmurs.

"I just…" Everything clogs up in my throat. Another touch draws my stinging gaze to Dad. His hand presses to the side of my head, sliding down to cup the back of my neck and pull me away from Mom and into his arms.

I grab on to him, releasing a shuddering breath into his shoulder.

"It's okay, Rem."

That makes it not okay, and moisture finally forces its way from my eyes. Mom's hand presses beside Dad's in the space between my shoulders.

"Dad?" Blair's voice, compressed and scared, barely draws my head up. Dejan is poised in the kitchen doorway, apology on his face. Blair latches on to my leg and tries to climb up between Dad and me.

I give in and pick him up. He leans back in my arms, hands pressed to my cheeks, seeing the redness in my eyes and feeling the dampness on my skin. Then he hugs me, small arms around my neck. I hold him there, trying to at least get my breathing under control.

"Do you have to go away again?" he asks into my shoulder.

"I don't know, Bear." I look to my parents. "But there's going to be some people around for the next few days. Cieran, Besim, and Dej will probably be here too."

"Why?"

So he didn't understand too much. Good.

"You know how we usually go fight bad guys somewhere else?"

His hair tickles the side of my neck with his nod. "Are they coming here?"

"Might be. We're just trying to keep everyone safe."

He pulls back. "Who's going to keep you safe?"

"We look out for each other, Bear," Dejan says. He's watching me from the sideways glance I throw, not able to look fully at him.

"Okay." Blair gets that. But my parents are less convinced.

"There's going to be a briefing, and a team of BMA agents will be around," I say.

"We get a say in the house being taken over?" Dad grumbles.

"It's just for a few days." Hopefully. But I also need to tell Cieran about the magpie. We need that briefing sooner, and I'm not about to leave the house with the threat of her close by.

I loosen my hold on Blair and he slides back down to the ground, but the look he turns up at me is still concerned.

I ruffle his hair and give him a smile. "Sorry for scaring you."

"It's okay. Can we read?"

"Yeah. Go find our book."

He slowly disappears.

"Dej, will you contact Cieran and catch him up?" My voice is mostly even again. Dejan technically outranks me as squad corporal, but if I try to pull out my phone and talk about any of this, I might lose it again.

The elf strides forward to grip my shoulder. I almost can't meet his gaze.

"We've got you, Rem." One shake, and then he's gone from the kitchen, heading to the front room to call Cieran. But the words break against me. Maybe it's just a token phrase he's saying, and I've already lost some of his trust.

I face off with my parents again.

"You've been different ever since then," Mom starts carefully. "That why?"

I nod, afraid to talk and fully admit to the horrifying shame of being targeted and used for someone's purpose. Suddenly learning I was a father from it had been another brutal check from life. She sighs, and there's a watery glint in her eyes.

She touches my arm again. "What do you need from us?"

"There'll be some Agents around. Just don't be extra stubborn, stay safe, and help me keep an eye on Bear."

Dad cracks his knuckles. "Don't worry. I'll be ready."

It gets a faint smile. There's a warrior in there somewhere. "Thanks, Dad."

His hands drop on my shoulders, and he gently rocks me back and forth, nodding solemnly. My mom looks like she's about to start sharpening her paring knives. She's five-foot-three and usually more interested in micro-flora, but Dad and I have always known not to piss her off.

"Whatever you need, Remy. We're here for you and Bear."

It draws this exhausting feeling back. But I just nod, pushing it back down, because there's a mission ahead and I'm not going to let my family get hurt.

5

REMY

My arms cross back over my chest, shielding myself as I make my way to the living room. Bear's still trying to track down the book he probably doesn't remember bringing to my room last night.

Dejan affirms something and slides his phone away before turning to me. "Cieran's coming as soon as he gets his gear. He's re-routing Besim here."

I force myself to look at him, but falter with his quiet, "You okay?"

"Yeah," I scoff at my boots.

"Rem."

But I shake my head. Fates, this is worse. With Cieran it hurt, but it wasn't so bad because he doesn't know me. Not the way Dejan and Besim do. And it's got me feeling like I'm sixteen again, back for a visit to the Islands. Not quite fitting in because my accent isn't exactly right when I speak Hawaiian, and unable to stuff the hurt inside when I'm too *haole* for some. Time away from the islands, the bit of Britannica blood, and years of American living blamed.

Accepted by others, but still asked why I'm not moving there as soon as I'm eighteen. I've got aunts and uncles and cousins to spare. Especially after spending summers to train with the native warlocks, learning the ways of our magic. The disappointment when I always return to the States, always trying to find where I fit.

And Crew Six is that place, the first group I felt in step with, equals with. Family, brothers. And because I was stupid years ago, it might be lost.

"Rem," he says again, patient. "I never liked her." He breaks the silence that I keep.

It draws a faint laugh. They met her once. Weeks before it happened.

"You don't like anybody." I raise my head.

Dejan shrugs. "I like you, *shilsa*."

"Language." I lift my chin. He glances guiltily over his shoulder, checking to make sure Bear hasn't come back out.

"Why do you think this is going to change that?" he asks.

I shake my head, arms squeezing tighter over my chest.

"It didn't change you." His tone is still quiet, borderline "therapy voice." But I can't manage to jokingly call him Besim, because his words are hitting as part of me still argues them.

I scoff again, scuffing a boot against the tile.

"Not in any way that matters." Dejan comes a step closer. If I didn't know better, he looks like he's about to hug me, but that's my thing and he's not so big on physical touch.

I'm fighting the lump in my throat so I still don't answer.

He huffs. "You going to make me punch you?"

I finally do laugh, faint and a little strangled, but it's there. And with it, I settle back into the sense of belonging, knowing they're not going to give up on me yet. He does hug me, maybe trying to shock me again. He slaps my shoulder and taps the side of his head against mine before he steps back.

"Thanks," I say a little thickly.

Dejan just nods. "Go gear up. She's going to get a fight."

6

SARA

LUNCH IS NOT MEANT to be. I wait through the entire line at the food truck, order, and have taken one bite of delicious spicy beef-filled naan when my phone buzzes. I fumble wrap, tablet, and folders to dig it from the pocket of my fitted jeans.

Fortin. "Change of plans. Get to the Specialist's house right now."

"What happened?" I haven't managed to swallow my bite yet, so it's a mumbled mess.

"Ballagh has apparently been watching him for a while and just made a threat."

"Oh." I almost drop everything along with a curse.

"I'll be there as soon as I can. We're moving the briefing up to as soon as everyone's there."

"Yes, ma'am." I look ruefully at my wrap, because it's not going to survive the trip.

"Sara." Her voice softens for a moment. "Be careful."

"I will." I respond with a cheeriness I don't feel. Because this is turning out exactly the way she wanted it to. Forcing the agent perfectly happy with data analysis into the field position. I toss the wrap into the nearest waste can. Thinking about being a field agent killed my appetite anyway.

I pull up the city map on my tablet and input Remy's address, shaking my head and trying to remember to call him Specialist. *Be professional.* It's not far, so I start my best powerwalk, trying to remember the training—check your surroundings, have a hand ready for the knife at all times—it takes some more juggling to keep a secure handle on the tablet and folder since I didn't think I'd need a bag today. Ha. That'll teach me.

Keep some distance between you and others at all times. Pretty sure these instructions weren't meant for crowded city sidewalks.

Eventually I give up and just walk. I've lost focus trying to remember all these things and I've almost taken a wrong turn. I jog the last block, check the address one more time, and then walk up a short walkway lined by some of the brightest flowers I've ever seen to a sturdy wooden door inset in a red brick façade. Curtains are cracked open and a sense of waiting overlies the house.

Hesitation fills my knock, but the door swings open and I look up at a burly man with a bit of grey in his hair, and short sleeves exposing Islander tattoos. A frown creases his features. He looks like he usually smiles, so this expression is even scarier.

"Hi." I try not to lean back from it. "I'm Agent Sara Alder with the Bureau of Magical Affairs."

"How do I know that?" he growls, Hawaiian accent lilting through.

"It's okay, Dad. You can let her in."

The man glances to his left though Remy's voice definitely came from further inside. I tentatively step in, and clutch my tablet to my chest with a faint yelp at the elf standing right inside the door with knife drawn.

His cold stare hasn't changed from the sidewalk outside the command tower. He slowly sheathes the knife, nudges me forward, and closes the door.

"Agent." Remy's voice draws my attention into the cozy living area filled with overstuffed couches, bright rugs, and more plants. They're spilling off the mantle, clustered in pots with bright geometric paintings, and hanging in front of windows.

I like it.

He's changed into dark grey trousers, calf-high boots, and there's a glint of silver as he straps on a heavy vest. It takes a second to realize it's a mail shirt under a dark short-sleeved fatigues shirt. I've never seen mail up close. Police just have standard-issue tac vests, and thankfully as an analyst, I've never had to work with the Bureau's special response team. They're...intense.

"I'm assuming you got the update?" Remy asks.

I jolt a little from the question, realizing I've been awkwardly staring. "Yes. Sounds like my boss is coming this way too."

He pulls belts from the bag on the couch and starts strapping knives to his thighs, and another across his chest. "Don't touch that, Bear."

Confusion reigns until he moves and exposes the child curled on the couch, peering into his bag with interest.

"Dad, I want to see the rock sword."

"Basalt. Look, don't touch." It's a gentle reminder, a little at odds with the transformed warrior standing in the living room.

I can't help but smile at the sight of the kid, now on his knees, peering into the bag. He's got a thatch of dark hair, and bright, curious eyes when he looks back at Remy.

Another knock sends me jolting, but it has an odd rhythm to it. I spin to see the elf cracking it open. But his knife is not out. A towering figure steps through and I back up a step. The elf throws the deadbolt, taps the newcomer on the shoulder, then heads around the couch.

"I'll be back," he tells Remy, fist-bumps the little boy, and vanishes through the back of the house.

"You must be one of the agents." The newcomer's voice is *deep* but kind.

I manage to free a hand to shake, feeling like I'm looking up at a skyscraper to meet his gaze. "Agent Sara Alder."

"Besim Antilles."

And I finally catch the hilt of a longsword over his shoulder, at odds with the jeans and dusty work shirt. He looks like he just came from a construction site. A bag is slung over his shoulder, and I'm assuming it's gear like Remy's.

"Do you have a rank I'm supposed to call you?"

His smile gentles his blocky features, the thick jaw, and a bit of warbled looking skin streaking his left cheek and down his neck. "No, I'm Communications Specialist, but we don't normally get hung up on rank."

I nod, filing it away. "Nice to meet you."

He nods, and heads around the couch to tap Remy's shoulder with a heavy fist. There's some unspoken communication between them, then Besim turns to the boy. "Hey, Bear."

"Bes!" The boy stands up on the couch, extending arms up, and Besim obliges, juggling the kid, his large bag, and sword like they're nothing. He's got to be part troll from his size.

"Cir is on the way," Besim tells Remy. The warlock is more at ease here in his military gear and surrounded by his crew.

"Is there somewhere I can stay out of the way?" I ask.

Their focus draws to me, and the boy cranes his head to look from where he's slung over Besim's shoulder.

"Yeah." Remy pauses for a second to take the kid from Besim before the soldier disappears, probably to go change from street clothes.

The boy squirms onto Remy's back, and he loosens the kid's grip around his neck as he comes around the couch that separates the living area from the entryway. "Kitchen will be fine."

I follow him, winking at the boy who still peers at me in curiosity. He blinks back, a faint little grin in place.

"Are you one of the people we have to be nice to?" he asks.

A sigh cuts from Remy, but I chuckle. "Only if you want to. I'm Sara."

"Blair."

"Blair?" I repeat, trying to make sure I heard it correctly since I was definitely hearing *Bear* a second ago.

Remy half-turns. "Bear's a family name."

Even if his voice wasn't suddenly a little too even and deep, I'm not that socially isolated behind a desk piled high with computer and folders that I can't read between the lines. Blair it is.

The kitchen is through another door—a wide room, light green cabinets contrasting white tile floor. A rack on the wall is filled with a mix of mugs, which judging from size and color variety, have been collected on travels. An older woman sits at the well-worn wooden table, a mug in hand.

"Mom, this is Agent Alder."

The woman sends a faint smile to Remy with his package who seems very pleased to be getting a lift from his dad. She stands and leans over the table to extend her hand. "Rebecca Kalama."

She's lighter skinned than her son and wavy hair is contained in a loose braid, bits of grey frosting the dark. Laugh lines creased deep around her eyes have been smoothed a little in concern. And now that she's standing, I've got at least a few inches on her. It's rare that I feel tall.

"Sara Alder."

"Welcome. Set your things wherever you need." Rebecca gestures around the kitchen and I take the corner opposite her, setting down my things and easing into the chair.

"Thanks."

"Need anything? Tea? Coffee?" she asks. There's a hint of a Britannic accent in her words, and it makes for an oddly comforting cadence.

"Just water would be great." I'm not about to ask for food because now I'm here, I'm regretting tossing my wrap.

"Dad, can we read yet?" Blair wiggles, trying to climb over Remy's shoulder to peer into his face.

"As soon as Cieran gets here," Remy reassures.

"When is he getting here?"

"Don't know, Bear. Soon."

I smile thanks at Rebecca as she hands me a glass of ice water.

"Can you watch him for a few minutes?" Remy asks his mom, and she nods with a look of understanding, taking Blair off Remy's back.

"Come help me make lunch. Agent, you want anything?"

"Oh, I don't want to intrude." But my stomach is about two seconds from rumbling again and I swallow some water like that'll fill it up.

"It won't be," she says somewhat wryly. "I'm about to feed Besim and Cieran together, so another on top of them won't be a bother."

I chuckle. Remy has backed away, one more glance at Blair as if making sure he'll be okay with me in the room, and vanishes.

"Can I help with anything?" I ask.

Rebecca shakes her head, and starts pulling things from the refrigerator. Low voices come from the living room. I fiddle with my tablet for a minute or so—feeling very out of place—before I open it up and start poking through some work that has been piling up with my recent focus on the Ballagh case. The small notepad I carry around to keep my hands busy with notes or doodles comes out and I'm twirling a pen around my fingers, losing myself in the numbers and data points.

I should probably be trying to talk to everyone, getting a feel for the house and any specific relations to Ballagh, but like I said, I'm an analyst resisting my boss's push toward field agent. As long as she's not here, I can pretend I'm not on some sort of one-sided experimental run.

A rustle pulls me from my work. Blair carefully sets down a small cookie-laden plate on the table before climbing up onto a chair. He pushes the plate over.

"I made these with Dad. They're super good." He kneels on the chair, arms leaning on the table, watching me as I take a bite.

"You did a really good job." I grin around the mouthful of chocolate cookie. Oh man, this might turn into a halfway decent assignment.

He beams back. "What's your favorite cookie?" he asks.

I'm tempted to say the one I'm finishing off, but that might look like I'm being a suck-up. "Peanut butter. What about you?" I dust my hands off.

"All cookies. But ones with sprinkles are really good."

I lean a little closer. "Sprinkles make everything better."

He chuckles, a deep sound for such a small body. His eyes light on my notepad. "You like to draw too!"

"Mostly doodle," I tell him.

He leans closer, tilting to look at my scribbles. "A dragon!" he whispers. "I can't do dragons very good. I want to draw Dad's, but it's too squiggly."

If there's a dragon in this house, I guess I wouldn't be surprised.

"Here." I flip to a clean sheet, risking a look around. Rebecca has one eye on us, and she offers a small smile. I'm not reading concern, but I'm mostly looking for Remy to make sure this would be okay. "What kind of dragon should we draw?"

We collaborate, which is way more fun than looking at numbers until they go fuzzy. It obviously needs color, but I'm forced to admit I don't have my usual bag with me, so there's no colored pencils to pull out. Drawing is usually my reset on long days when I need a break from screens or numbers or when nothing is matching up the way it needs to.

"I'll get colors!" He scrambles down. "Dad, we're making a dragon!"

Startled, I glance up from shading a bit of the wings to see Remy leaning against the doorframe where he's clearly been keeping an eye on us. He doesn't move to stop Blair, or tell me different, so I sort of awkwardly smile and turn back to touching up some lines until Blair comes back with handfuls of markers clutched to his chest. They clatter onto the table and then he grabs Remy's hand and pulls him over.

"Does it look like...what's her name?" Blair cranes a look back at Remy once he reclaims the seat.

"Athina?" Remy arches an eyebrow, some amusement there.

"Yeah. 'Thina."

A faint smirk softens Remy's face. "You'll have to ask Cieran when he gets here."

Whatever that means.

Blair picks up a green marker. "I'll do the wings." He hands me blue. "You can do the face."

I uncap the marker, and dare to look up at Remy who still hasn't moved. "Uh, is there a dragon around I need to be aware of?"

I sound like I'm halfway joking, but I'm really not. Real dragons are few and far between, most killed off in the Middle Centuries or in deep hibernation like the magma dragons of the Hawaiian Islands for a hundred years or more. Which is why the dragons appearing over Dunhare eight months ago caused a pretty big stir.

He flashes another small smile. "No. We know a dragon shifter."

"You...?" My mouth drops open. "Those dragonwalkers eight months ago. That was your team?" The Bureau hadn't been involved, but *everyone* had heard about it.

"Yeah." He walks away without another word, just a ruffle to Blair's hair while the boy still colors.

Another knock comes from somewhere and the sergeant's voice sounds. Blair perks up. "Cieran!"

This kid has got a set of lungs on him. Voices rise and fall, then bootsteps thunk over. Blair twists in his chair. "Cieran, Dad said to ask you if this looks like 'Thina."

The sergeant comes over, changed into dark grey fatigues, the long sleeves rolled up to his elbows leaving chain mail exposed, the same boots as before now laced up over his trousers. And still the backwards hat. He definitely looks the part of the soldier like this. I'd been surprised when he was introduced as the commanding officer and not Remy when they came into the office.

"Hey, Agent," he greets me easily, and then leans over our drawing. A grin splits his face and I'm really worried what that might mean. "Looks pretty good, kiddo."

"What color is she?"

"Her scales are red, but one of her friends has green scales."

Blair turns to me. "Can we make another one after?"

"Sure." I hesitate, because everyone now showing up is making the reality of the case come back and pushing the fun little art session to the back burner.

"Bear." Remy's low voice interrupts. He shakes his head a little, and Blair's shoulders slump. "Leave the agent alone."

"It's okay," I hasten to say. "This is more fun than anything else I could be doing while we wait for everyone."

"Okay." But there's still hesitation in the specialist. He points at his son. "Don't pester."

Blair nods, but he's already coloring again. Cieran nudges the boy's head down and Blair grins at him as he and Remy step back out.

7

REMY

BESIM EMERGES FROM THE bathroom in fatigues and light thermal and drops his bag on the couch to dig out chain mail.

"We're having the briefing here?" he asks.

I swallow hard and force myself closer. "Yeah."

He immediately locks on to me, forgetting the armor. "What's going on?" *With you?* The rest is clear.

Trolls all look human except for a grey skin tone and matching toughness that rivals granite. Besim is half, and has tanned human skin from his mom's side. But when we're in combat, he can call up the troll stoneskin to cover his body and give him more protection than our armor. He's our Communications Specialist, all things tech his specialty. I've seen him jury-rig a radio with half-burned parts in the middle of an ambush to call for backup.

But despite all this and the troll blood that most think would make him a pretty aggressive soldier, he's the opposite. Oh, he's efficient in a fight and there's no one else I want on my flank, but he's team mom and is quicker with a quiet word of reassurance or advice than he is with the sword.

It really shook Dejan and me when Besim was clearly struggling six months ago with his own trauma following the Wastelands mission and the wild magic that ate *through* his stoneskin to leave the scarring down his entire left side.

He's also more religious than any of us, and that small saint medal he keeps on his ident tag chain makes it feel like the one guy who's definitely not going to judge me, actually might.

"Rem?"

And just like that, the soft "therapy voice" that Dejan and I complain about but don't mind at all because it gets us talking when we'd rather bottle it all up inside, comes out. I offer a faint smile that's definitely a few degrees south of humor.

He doesn't say anything as I tell him, voice pitched low to avoid drawing attention from the kitchen. And doesn't say anything for an eternal five heartbeats after I finish.

"And you're feeling guilty about something you had no control over," he states.

I shake my head, pinning him with a frustratedly angry look. "Maybe I could have."

"But you didn't." The gentle words hit me so hard in the chest that I have to turn my head away for a moment.

"Remy." His fist taps my shoulder. I clear my throat in a telling way, before managing to look at him. "You didn't have to tell me, but thanks."

The "yeah, I did," sticks. It was going to come out in one way or another, but some part of me is glad people around me know and nothing has changed except them pulling closer.

"And hey." He jostles me. "You love Bear. Nothing made you do that. You're a good dad."

I've loved him since the moment I held a tiny, swaddled, and screaming Bear to my chest and he instantly fell asleep. Despite the way he came into my life, there was nothing like that moment, and a lot of other moments since.

But Besim's words are more difficult to believe when Blair's mother is coming back and planning nothing good. Her words echo back through the harsher edge of the magpie. *I want you again.*

My skin crawls and I slide out from under Besims's grip. He's not judging, neither are Dejan or Cieran, but that's not stopping me from replaying it all over and over, worsening with each telling. I shut off the part of myself that got broken with her actions years ago. And maybe it can't be fixed.

"Rem?" Besim questions.

But I just nod. "Thanks." I turn away, knowing that he's not fooled at all. He'll be around, closer if needed to help me keep myself from breaking any more than I already have.

I make my way back to the kitchen, leaving him to arm up, and keep his reassurances to himself for now. I don't want to think or do anything other than keep Bear and my family safe.

Agent Alder sits close to Blair. So close that I almost lurch over there and pull him away. It takes another second to register that they're so close because she's drawing something and he, in typical Bear fashion, is enthralled, halfway onto the table watching.

I listen to their conversation and his suggestions for some creature I *think* is a dragon. And she's humoring him every time. I wish he had more stranger danger, but he makes friends everywhere he goes. Maybe he hasn't noticed yet that I never take him around a lot of strangers, and we stick to known places, and I don't like anyone other than the team and my parents' friends over.

Mom pauses beside me. "He's okay," she whispers. I slant a look at her and that same understanding is there. I feel like she's cataloguing every action that I have or haven't taken in the last five years and reframing.

"I'll keep an eye on him," she reassures before moving away.

And when Alder realizes that I'm standing there, she just offers an awkward smile, and something about that reassures me more than any words. Elves, and definitely half-elves, don't have glamour, so she's not literally hiding her true expression. From the brief interactions we've had, she doesn't seem like she's got any ulterior motives yet. And even if she did, no one can fake being that uncomfortable with weapons. Which might end up being more of a threat later if combat comes. But for now, I'll let her and Bear color since it's keeping both of them occupied and in eye-line.

I'll figure out how to watch him later after the briefing and the plan gets set.

8

SARA

REBECCA BRINGS US GRILLED sandwiches, stacked with turkey and melted cheese. We both juggle eating and coloring, and this is definitely better than playing field agent and still trying to ignore the reasons I don't want to take the transfer.

Analyst is easier, safer. Harder to let anyone down. I've spent half of my life in the broad shadow of my full-elf brother who's got magic and charisma and the focus of my mom and stepdad. I guess along the way I stopped trying and just stick to what I know and what I know I'm good at.

The feeling I've had since Fortin placed folders on my desk, a gleam in her eyes announcing she'd finally found the excuse to get me into the field, has only gotten worse. This is going to turn to something messy if we're not careful, and I don't want to let anyone down, especially this Specialist and his team. Mostly for the sake of this little boy gleefully coloring my drawing.

Blair and I make another dragon, and I'm a little worried about whoever this Athina person is and if she'll be offended by my dragons since my only references are centuries-old art and some street graffiti.

He wheedles some more cookies for us and I shamelessly accept. And every time I look up, Remy seems to be there, keeping an eye on us.

Guess I can't blame him, based on what I know about Ballagh and some other details of the case. She's full fae. What some might call High Fae due to her purple eyes. Grey is the most common eye color, but purple means direct descent from Celtica and Britannic Fae. And usually means incredibly powerful magic. Those countries drew fae from all over and hosted the Courts. It's been debated what the Courts actually were, since they were destroyed in the earlier Middle Centuries. That broke the Fae's oppressive power and started to disperse them back across the earth.

But what we do know is that there was, still is to some extent, something about Celtica, Britannica, even Hibernia that held vast reservoirs of natural magic, and something that amplified it. Ley lines, standing stones, no one really knows.

Fae soak up wild magic from all around them, their genetics acting as a natural refinery for the sometimes volatile natural magic, and use it to cast. If, on the odd chance, they're somewhere without natural magic, then they have no casting ability. Those places are incredibly rare, and usually only occur after someone's done a large casting in the area and drained the immediate reservoirs. The magic will usually grow back, but it takes generations.

The Courts breaking actually put limitations on fae. Four-hundred-year lifespan instead of near immortality. Access to magic kept their bodies regenerating almost constantly. It's why elves usually live longer too, with their inherent natural magic of *regeneration* and *nurture.* No more ability to shapeshift except in rare cases. Glamour only to minimally modify appearance. Not as susceptible to iron which is a natural magic repellent. But it can still really burn according to the fae I know.

Still really good with animals and nature, and some minor power over names and actions.

In the case of magic and glamour, Maeve Ballagh is incredibly strong. She's at least two hundred years old. The math gets complicated when trying to adapt that to human years. Especially when fae tend to still look kind of ageless. Personally I think it's the glamour they can still use. Some run whole businesses and sell anti-aging charms to reduce lines and wrinkles. She clearly has really good control over nature with using that magpie as a go-between. Not many can project voices through animals anymore.

And every guy has basically started drooling when we've talked to them about her. She's probably using some low-level attraction spells along with glamour to get them to ignore any wife or girlfriend they have to sleep with her. Everyone except Remy. He had almost the exact opposite reaction. I risk a glance at him. He's still on guard, deceptively relaxed.

Ballagh doesn't really seem to care about getting pregnant since she seems to have dropped kids off with all of them. Something about that really bothers me, especially after the traffickers in custody kept saying that she was interested in the kids they had and kept "testing" their magic somehow.

That and the other papers she left behind are creating a puzzle that I'm not sure I want to solve. Especially in light of her coming back and finding the other men she has kids with.

We have to put arts and crafts on hold once Fortin arrives and the kitchen table turns into the briefing center. Besim has changed. A new bulkiness covers the half-troll with his tac vest, fatigue sleeves also rolled to his elbows, and dark bracers strapped to his forearms.

A faint rustle announces a newcomer and I jolt to see the elf back and in full gear as well. He's leaning against the doorframe and smirks slightly when he sees he has my attention. He gets introduced as Corporal Dejan Kostic, and gives a slight lift of his head, crossing his arms over his bow, archer's brace covering the part of his mail shirt that the short-sleeved fatigues don't.

I try not to be intimidated by the guys in their full gear standing around while the sergeant sits. Remy's dad hangs back behind the counter. I guess no one is going to tell him he can't be there when it's his house. Rebecca has vanished with Blair, who had to be carried out after trying to stay with his dad.

"Okay, Agent Alder, let's get started." Fortin places clasped hands on the table. Her look at Remy has him slowly sitting down with us.

I square up my tablet and notebook to the edge of the table and take a short breath. "Like we said earlier, we've been tracking Ballagh for some time. She's been brought in for some petty thefts but been able to walk every time. Over time, looks like she's progressed into larger scale artifact thefts and then into trafficking. She hasn't been caught for those yet, but fingerprints, witnesses, and other accomplices have put her on scene."

I've been compiling an almost forty-year-long criminal dossier on her over the last few months, and she's been dabbling in almost everything you could imagine.

"With the most recent raid on the traffickers' safe house, we got more of a breakthrough. It looks like she's got her own agenda around helping traffic kids with magic. It has to do with the list of names we found, including Specialist Kalama's."

The soldiers are all scowling, and Mr. Kalama crosses his arms.

"The other men also have kids." I'm sort of *not* looking at Remy. "All the men have magic of some sort, and all have a story of her disappearing and then coming back and leaving a child with them."

Remy sinks back into his chair, shoulders curling up. There's a slight shift in the room and his companions are all a little closer and more protective.

"As far as we know, none of the kids have magic, and she doesn't seem to be interested in the children, just the men."

"Why?" the elf interrupts.

Sergeant O'Donnell tips a glance back at him that's borderline reprimanding, but he turns the same question to me a second later.

"Given that the men didn't really remember their last interaction with her, they couldn't give much of an answer. One did state that he noticed his family genealogy out the next day and couldn't remember why he'd been looking through it. If that's something she made him do in order to look at it, she hasn't checked back in. That was a few weeks ago. It was a change in the pattern that we thought was interesting. Any thoughts, Specialist?"

Even though I'd been given permission to call him Remy, Fortin is big on titles and probably won't appreciate the casual use of first names.

His hands fiddle with each other and he doesn't answer for a second. A gruff clearing of a throat precedes his father stomping over and yanking out a chair to sit next to him. His arms cross, and Fortin and I get a glower.

Remy rolls his eyes slightly, and finally speaks. "When she made contact today, she just said that she 'wanted me again.' She gave until tonight for me to decide different than 'hell no.'" He shrugs. "Didn't say much else."

"Um…" I cough, face heating. "Before, did she seem interested in anything about you or your family?"

The genealogy thing had stuck out to me, and I'd been digging into the others' lineages as much as I could. She's looking for *something* but I don't know why it would be in genealogies of different races. One's was locked due to government positioning, and I assume Remy's is likely to be guarded due to his service in the Army's special forces branch, but maybe I can just get the cliff notes from them.

A motion runs through him that if I didn't know better, I might think he was squirming from the question.

"When she introduced herself, it was because she'd seen my warlock tattoos and asked about them."

Okay, so that was pretty much just sounding like it was targeting magic users like the others. Not all warlocks have marking tattoos, but generally stronger magic users can sense magic in others. Fortin has said that she can identify other warlocks based on some low-level signal their magic all gives off. Fae and elves can sometimes do the same. Human genes balanced out my elvish genes a little too much and I don't have very much access to magic.

"Did she say anything about Blair when she brought him?" It comes soft from me, and I'm afraid of how the question might change the room.

Remy goes still and quiet, and there's something dangerous now, like I might be threatening the kid along with a crazy fae lady.

"Just that he wasn't what she *needed*." He spits the reply and I pull back a little.

What does that mean?

"Does he have any magic?" Fortin's practical voice cuts in. Maybe she can sense my slight panic at angering a room full of Drax Guard soldiers and one very intimidating house owner.

"No."

"Are you sure? He's what...three?"

She's poking and no one is happy. I'm ready to grab my tablet and dive out of the way.

Remy gives her an even look. "Four. I've tested him myself. And since I was pulling fire from candles at nine months old, if he had any as my son and as a half-fae, it would have shown by now."

Fortin inclines her head. Accepting the response. Although my eyes are a little wide as I look to Remy. Nine months old? Most don't start showing until two or three years at least. How powerful is he?

But he's right. Fae genetics usually overpower anything, and since all fae have magic, that means any offspring is going to have some sort of magic. Eye color will tell you more. Any half-fae has a band of bright purple or grey from their fae parent around their iris.

"Has magic always run in your line?" Fortin's question goes to the elder Kalama.

He leans back in the chair and it adds an aggressive creak to the conversation. "Yes. We come from the islands where the first dragons came from the volcanoes. It's passed through males in our line. Although it is not often used now as Remy does."

For war. Fire magic had its place when wooden ships came to conquer, quickly discovering that they were not equipped to go up against magma dragons and fire-wielding warriors. It's a wilder and more untamed magic than those who live on continents that didn't have native dragons. Warlocks usually come from places with dragons, or some sort of geologic feature like volcanoes, canyons, immense waterfalls. Anything where natural magic pools and then seeps into anything living to affect DNA.

This seems to be something contentious between them given the way Remy shoots a look at his father, and the way the elf and Besim seem to loom as backup again for Remy. No doubt they're thankful for his grasp of fire and wild magic.

"We haven't quite narrowed down what about the other men's magic line would have attracted her yet. Our research team has been working with Agent Alder on it but so far nothing," Fortin says. "But it is odd that all these children who should have magic, don't."

If she's about to suggest testing Blair in some way to see if he actually does have magic, I really am going to duck for cover.

"So we grab Ballagh and ask her ourselves." Sergeant O'Donnell shrugs.

"It might not be that easy," Fortin warns.

Cieran leans crossed arms on the table, hands close enough to his vest for one thumb to hook around the bulky hilt of a sheathed knife. "Agent, I'm not about to let some fae wreak havoc on one of my team or target someone else. We don't make it to the Drax Guard because we sit around on our asses. We're here to make a plan and put a stop to this. You've got most of the background info, so let's get started on that. I don't really care what her schemes are right now. I've got a soldier and a kid to keep safe and that's my mission objective."

The sort of easygoing vibe he had is gone, even with the hat still backwards. Sharpness lines his eyes and the laughter has vanished. *Don't piss him off.*

Fortin gives him a respectful nod. She understands most of the sentiment. "Okay. She made it clear she's coming here tonight with some sort of final ultimatum for Specialist Kalama."

Looking at the four soldiers, I can understand why Ballagh's maybe moving a little more carefully with Remy instead of just showing up.

"Moving now might trigger an early attack or send her into the wind, and I'm not risking Rem's family beyond this house," Cieran says. "From what she told Remy when she made contact, sounds like she's been watching this place for a while. Odds are, she's seen us all come in. We stake out the house." Cieran acts like it's already decided.

"I do want to try for capture, not kill," Fortin says. "She's going to be a gold mine of information on other trafficking rings."

The grimness sharpens around the sergeant's eyes again. Even I know about that bit of their reputation. If they can't capture, the alternative is lethal.

"We'll keep that in mind, Agent, but no promises." He sits back. "And I'm taking point, so let whatever other team you've got coming know that."

Fortin looks like she might argue, and I'm ready to use my tablet as a shield, but Cieran is not moving.

"You don't trust the Agency, Sergeant?" she asks. Normally I'd be right there with her, bristling at the implication that our teams are less than up for the task, but seeing these guys makes me think that our response teams are the C team at the very best.

"Not with this."

There's another bit of a stare down, but at least it's not crackling with as much *danger*.

Fortin relents and nods. "You've got point on security, Sergeant, but I'm running everything else."

"Fine."

I'd expected some more resistance from the sergeant, but the soldiers are all already shifting like they're ready to move out. Maybe they are.

Cieran pushes back his chair. "Dej, get outside and find some height."

The elf nods and vanishes through the door with barely a rattle of his quiver.

"Rem, get some more wards up around the house. Besim, watch his six."

They nod and disappear as well. He turns to Mr. Kalama, and this time there's a faint smile. "Keahi, can I get some coffee?"

Mr. Kalama smiles, instantly changing him into something gentler and not a volcano about to blow. "Sure, Cieran. What else am I doing?"

"I'm putting you in charge of Bear and Rebecca. Remy might not be able to cover them if something happens. I need magic ready to go." Cieran's hands brace on the back of the chair, and he steadily regards Keahi. It seems like an argument the sergeant has heard before and there's some affront in the man's returning posture.

Then, Keahi's broad shoulders relax, his features gentling with wry admission. "I never much liked Remy using his magic the way he does. But now that my family is threatened and my boy is in the crossfire, I'm finding little reason to not light everything on fire."

A grin quirks Cieran's lips. "That's what I want to hear. But keep it tight until you get a signal from me, or if someone outside this confirmed team is coming at you with a weapon."

Keahi nods, standing and moving into the main kitchen area to pull out mugs and a coffee pot from a cabinet.

"Okay." Cieran turns to us. His hand sneaks up to tap at his ear, and I hadn't even marked the comm he had there. "What else do I need to know about this fae?"

9

Remy

It's been one hour. One hour, and it feels like days. I've never liked waiting and I don't know how I'm going to get through the rest of the day. The house has never seemed this small, never felt crowded with the crew around. Though we've never been in gear and that seems like it's taking more space than anything.

Bear's restless. I told him to leave Alder alone three times because she needs to work and I'm still not comfortable with him being around either of the agents. He's been told he can't go outside twice in the last ten minutes, and the task of rearranging food storage containers with Grandma is not going to last long.

"Hi, excuse me."

I jerk from where I've been staring unseeing through the crack in the blinds and focus on Alder.

She holds the tablet against her chest under crossed arms, almost like a shield. And I'm doubtful again of this "field" agent and whatever she's going to be doing if weapons are pulled. Alder shifts back imperceptibly, straightening, and it seems like she's gearing up in front of me. So maybe I didn't try to keep that thought off my face.

"Um." She clears her throat and shifts the tablet around. "We still don't have a solid lead on why she's targeting you or the others. But I just got the full case file sent over, and wanted to run some things by you, see if you could help us put anything together?"

Cieran's at my side in a second, reading the way my shoulders immediately stiffen, or maybe just catching the quick whiff of smoke as my magic flares hot and bright in my chest, ready to defend. I cross my arms over my chest, tucking palms flat against the vest straps at my sides. She glances toward my hands, and her face creases in apology.

"Sure," I say, voice wobbling. Fates, I haven't lost control this easily since I was in grade school and growth spurts were throwing everything out of whack.

But Alder looks to Cieran like she wants confirmation or the go-ahead, swiping a finger across the tablet when she gets it. "These are scans of the papers that she left behind after the safe-house raid."

I take the tablet and start skimming through, Cieran angling his head to see.

"This looks like math?" He jabs a finger at one picture to pause me, but I've already tapped the picture to get it a little bigger.

"It's a spell formula." I rotate the tablet. Numbers and runes march across the page, some in a discernible formula and others sporadically tumbling about.

"Do you know what it's for?" Alder asks. It sounds like she might know and this is some sort of test.

But one I'm going to fail. Warlocks don't really write down our spells or castings. A lot is verbal and physical, especially mine which comes from deeply rooted Hawaiian heritage. Many of the physical motions, especially in attack spell forms, can be found in the Ha'a war dances, or is tied to the language itself.

This stuff is taught more in university for magic users wanting to get a wizard degree in some specific kind of casting or magic use.

"I recognize some things." I point at a few numbers. "Input, rating strength or amount of magic." Every spell has some variations to control the amount of magic or energy to put into it. The bigger the spell, the bigger the energy cost, and if you don't prep right, you can end up using too much. Best case, you end up with one hell of a headache. Worst case in a coma until your magic starts to regenerate. If there was anything left to regenerate. "Couple of these runes are standard, but that's about all I got."

Alder bites at her lower lip. "We've had some of our top-rated agents look at it. Most are wizards. Even the ones with three degrees aren't exactly sure what she's trying to do." She leans over and flips to another picture. "She seems to be closer with this one."

This one has new symbols, some inserted into the same combinations as before. And three different places were circled and underlined, then connected to each other with lines.

"Agent Timball seems pretty sure she's trying to store massive amounts of energy into a nonspecific object or container—he keeps saying conduit—and then use that to...and this is where he's lost most of us...*fix* something?" Alder shrugs. "But there's no notes, no indication of what that might be."

"How much magic?" Cieran hooks his hands into the collar of his vest.

I home in on a number following an equal sign in one of the circled areas. I can read that fine, and that number can't be right.

Alder's hands curl over each other. "We're talking...huge, like"—her hands part for a moment—"like a sun, huge."

"Damn." Cieran sounds impressed.

"What's she going to use to contain that?" I ask and get another shrug.

Well, not surprising given how much they didn't know already. I keep swiping through. No schematics, no maps, nothing to solidify what she's been working on or what she wants it for.

"You said you knew her for a couple months?" Alder doesn't seem to have any other expression than apologetic, and it's starting to grate on me.

"Yeah."

"Most—all—of the others seemed to be more one-night stands. Brief flings at the very least." Alder's shoulders are rising up to her ears. "Since you knew her longer, was there anything she might have mentioned or done...?" She trails off.

My fingers tingle, wanting to release the pent-up magic shaking in my veins. Only the temperature rising and the fact that I'm holding her tablet gets me to twist my right heel against the floor, grounding me and helping my magic pull back to my center. Don't need to fry her electronics because she asked a question she doesn't realize the answer to.

I knew Ballagh longer because I made her work for it. The thought rips bitter through me. I swipe through the rest of the photos to buy myself some time, calm myself, though not sure how that's going to work while holding the case file that contains only a fraction of her misdeeds.

"Rem." Cieran's voice cuts through the anger boiling up again. He lifts the tablet from my hands and goes through it himself. "She linked to anyone other than the traffickers?"

Alder glances at me, and my hands tucking back to my sides. "No. Not yet anyway."

I'm dimly aware of them talking and Cieran asking more questions as I focus out the window again. What did I remember from five years ago? Besides warning signs and my own intuition that I smothered, just along for the thrill of dating someone like her. Besides that night.

Light glints off a suncatcher outside, one with stars dangling from a colorful circle. And it hits me.

"Fae Courts," I blurt. Their conversation stops. "She was obsessed with the fae Courts."

Her necklace, one I'd never seen her without, was a circle holding a rowan tree and a crescent moon positioned over the tree at the three o'clock. Ancient symbol of the High Fae Court.

"But the Courts haven't been around for centuries," Alder says. "Most fae who talk about the Courts just have some sort of weird romantic idea of them."

"That's for sure," Cieran mutters.

The Courts were destroyed and the fae seat of power was shattered in the fifth century, cutting their ability to directly draw almost limitless wild magic. It shortened their lifespans and broke the hold they had on Celtica and the Britannic Isle. Once the fae weren't in power, the Roman Empire was finally able to sweep in and a different age began.

"No, she'd done research on them, talked a couple times about the shattering." And the light in her purple eyes was, at the time, mesmerizing. Now, I'd definitely call it fanatic.

"Fix." Alder rocks back on her heels. "She wants to mend the shattering."

All three of us look at each other in disbelief. It took immense power to break the Courts, and it was only through one caster offering the entirety of his magic, and therefore his life, to do it and break the Fae's power.

And that's when I feel punched in the gut again.

"The kids." It whispers from me. Conduit. She's going to use a kid.

"*Fir.*" Cieran scrubs his jaw.

Alder's right there with him, face losing all color. "Are you sure?" It's weak, but she's already agreeing.

"She's not one to bring back the Courts and not enjoy it if she does. She's the type to set herself up as a queen. But she needs something to channel her power so she doesn't kill herself. She's trying to make a person into a conduit." I shake my head. And she's using men to get a kid.

"But she didn't take any of the kids back." Alder seems to perk up at that.

"Yeah." Cieran snaps his fingers. "You said Bear wasn't what she needed. So whatever she's doing hasn't worked yet."

But I need to sit down. What did she do to Bear? He doesn't have magic. He *should* have magic.

And she wanted *me*. Something I've been trying to ignore until it's staring me right in the face.

She wants another kid.

10

REMY

I CAN'T BREATHE. AND it's not until Cieran winces and yanks his earpiece out to dangle on its wire, and shakes me, that I realize *I'm* the reason I can't breathe. Whining feedback screams in my ear and I slam my palms together, cutting off the threatening heat wave.

The temperature falls and the comms cease fighting for their life against the magic buildup. Besim and his countermeasures are the only reason a lot of our tech survives me. Though usually, we only have to worry about it in combat situations.

"Whoa, hey, why is Remy casting?" Besim's voice cuts through.

I point to my ear and Cieran gets his comm tucked back in. "All good," he says.

"Sure? We felt that pressure dip out here." Dejan's Detroit accent comes through a lot stronger than normal. He's worried and about to jump down from whatever perch he's in and come find us.

"All good," I manage.

"Sounds like it," Dejan says wryly.

"I'm good," I say more firmly.

A huff answers and yeah, he doesn't believe me.

"Remy?" Mom appears in the living room, eyes wide and a container in hand like she's going to use the plastic as a weapon somehow.

"False alarm." My mouth barely moves in a smile. She also does not believe me with the way her brows still crease.

She darts a glance at the others, then speaks in Hawaiian. "You don't look okay."

But I don't answer her, because I'm registering the lack of a four-year-old who was with her. "Where's Bear?" I lurch forward a step, and Alder gives way.

"He's with your dad," Mom reassures but her features are still pinched in concern. "They're in the office."

"Remy." Cieran's hand taps my chest, stilling me before I can charge over there. "Take five. I'll go check on him, make sure he's okay. And I'll distract him for a bit." He gives a wry smile. "Not to brag, but I'm pretty good at Go Fish."

Something adjacent to a laugh huffs from me. "Thanks, Sarge."

His fist thumps my chest again and then he's gone, reassuring Mom on the way.

"Sorry," Alder apologizes. Again.

"Don't be sorry for doing your job," I tell her. Mostly because there's no way she can make this better and I need her to stop being sorry for it.

Her expression shifts and one brow lifts. "They honestly should have sent someone else, but my boss is trying to get me out of the analysts' office and into field work. I don't have much magic, and I must have skipped the 'how to deliver bad news' class when going through the Academy."

Her arms cross back over the tablet, and I unconsciously mirror her, palms pressing tight, making sure my magic stays at my center where it needs to be right now.

"I don't think there's really any good way to deliver this." I'm finally able to get myself to something sort of reassuring despite my stance. I don't smile, because I never talk to women outside of basic social niceties, don't give anyone any ideas. Which had made it so painful the entire months-long time that Besim's sister had a visible crush on me, but I couldn't ever manage to just tell her no.

"Yeah, just—"

I tilt my head, cutting off her sorry, and she flashes a small smile. I look away from it, right to the hanging plants that frame the window.

"Ah, crap." I sigh. She twists, following my rueful look at the withered and blackened leaves. Heat stress spots darken others. Mom might actually get mad at me for that.

Alder touches the trailing vines of the worst one, squinting her eyes, and then vibrant green rushes back, plumping out the leaves. It seems like every plant in the vicinity perks up and leans toward her.

"My tiny bit of elf magic." She shrugs like she's apologizing for that too. "About all I can do is heal some minor scrapes and bruises, and keep plants alive. Though I'm usually best with succulents."

"Don't let my dad hear you. He struggles with succulents," I say, then almost physically check myself. What am I doing? Like I'm inviting her past this professional relationship, letting anything about my family slip to a near stranger.

"They're like wild horses. Treat them with respect and don't look them in the eye."

A grin tugs my mouth and there's nothing but honesty in her face when she smiles back.

"Thanks for helping me not get in trouble with my mom." It slips out, loosening the tightness of my crossed arms with it, and a small part of me is horrified at myself.

Alder laughs, a low, clear sound, and it has mine trying to join until I snug my arms tight again.

"No problem. I know how important that is." But some tension fringes her smile, and she backs up, tapping a thumb against her tablet. "I need to go fill Fortin in. She might have some more questions later."

I nod, and as she steps away, I tap the earpiece. "I'm taking five."

Verbal affirmations come from all around, and I head to my room, sinking down on the bed with a sigh. I pull the earpiece out and leave it to dangle against the vest, turning the receiver volume up so I can hear if any update comes through.

I lean forward on my knees, scraping hands over my face and then through my hair, cupping around the back of my neck as I stare at the floor.

Most everything from my old apartment is still in boxes in the small shed out back. But Dad hasn't told me to clear it out yet—very unlike him—and it's been four years. That's left my room pretty sparse. Even as a teen, I had more stuff around. A few prized items like a signed Akamu Haoa poster, two-time Olympic gold medalist in fire-weaving from the Islands, always traveled from house to house, but it's packed away leaving a faintly darker rectangle on the wall where it used to hang.

Suddenly the bare walls feel like a pointed comment on how empty everything is, how much just *stopped*, as I've almost desperately kept myself cut off from a lot of things. Trying to control as much as I could.

"This what 'okay' looks like?"

I shake my head, lifting it to see Dejan leaning against the doorframe, thumbs hooked around his vest's shoulder straps. His comm dangles loose too.

"Is everyone taking five?" I ask.

"Don't worry, we've got some Bureau guys out back keeping an eye on things." The sardonic tone matches the roll of his eyes.

"Okay, great, we're all going to die." My huffing laugh joins his snicker.

"But seriously, Rem."

A sigh pushes my chest tight against my vest and I sit up, focused on my hands fiddling in my lap.

"Cir caught us up to speed on what you guys figured out," he says.

"Yeah." My jaw clenches. I don't know what's worse. That she targeted me, or she targeted me to get a kid who'd die when she throws all her magic through them to mend some ancient site.

"That's pretty *firred*."

A grin tugs against my will. "You've such a way with words."

Dej smirks as I finally look at him. "Besim might finally be rubbing off on me."

Oh definitely, Besim who I've heard curse a grand total of five times in the years of knowing him.

"What do you need?"

Well, I take it back. That's usually Besim's line, but he got both of us using it on him a few months back when he wasn't okay. I guess the lesson stuck with Dejan.

Heat builds in my chest again, and I'm not sure whether it feels like anger or shame. "To not feel like a *firren* piece of meat hung out to catch a predator."

Even as I say the last word, throat spasming around it, finally admitting that's what she was, that's what she did to me—the anger turns out to just be masquerading as humiliation, and it sends my magic turning away.

"Hey." Dejan's voice cuts sharp. "What did we all tell you?"

"Shit, Dej, she doesn't want Bear, she wants *me*." My face burns and I stare past him through the open door, down the short hall spilling into the living room with the plants that Alder brought back to life. "We should just leave, draw her out somewhere else."

"How do you know she's still not going to come after anyone here, use them as leverage?" he counters.

I don't. But I need to do something, to feel in control again. "Maybe we should just take the chance."

Dejan shakes his head. "People like her, people like..." His voice snags in a telling way. "You can run as far or as fast as you want, but that won't stop them from finding whatever or whoever you love first and sinking hooks in until you come crawling back begging. Waiting for her here doesn't make any damn sense, but it's the best way to try to control anything."

We all knew it. Didn't make that any easier to wait around until her deadline of "tonight." She'd rattled me like she probably intended, maybe hoping I'd push for something stupid and leave the others vulnerable. But she doesn't know Cieran. From the outside, he might seem to trend reckless with his snarky comebacks and the way he and his old team would plan pranks nonstop. But he's patient and methodical when running missions. He's not going to get riled. I trust him, but in this moment, if Bear or my parents were threatened, I'm really not sure that I'd listen to a direct order.

And that scares me too.

"Hey, if anything happens, we've all got your back." It's like Dejan can read my mind.

I draw in a breath, holding it, letting it fill up the farthest corners of my lungs. Tonight. I've made it through countless missions that all involved waiting. I can do it again.

"Besim got targeted six months ago, and now me. Anything you're not telling us?" I half-joke.

Dejan's attention flicks from me to the empty wall for another telling second. If there is something, I'm the poster child for not telling anyone about a past, so I'm not judging.

"Don't worry, I burned every bridge on my way out of Detroit." He lifts his chin with a thin smile, carelessly daring.

He doesn't talk about Detroit, his past, nothing but the last fifteen years of living in or around Dunhare. But sometimes we'll get almost hints, and it just never seems like there was anything good growing up in Detroit.

Bear tumbles through the door, dispelling the flash of emotions in Dejan's eyes—regret the loudest—as Bear latches on to his leg.

"Dejan, me and Cieran are playing cards. Can you come?"

He ruffles Bear's hair and pushes away from the door. "Sorry, kid. I need to get back outside. Rain check?"

"What's a rain check?"

Dejan puts the comm back in his ear. "Means I'll play with you next time I'm over. Sound good?"

But a frustrated growl rips through Bear and he stomps his feet, small arms stiffening by his sides. We're getting closer and closer to a full meltdown.

"Bear." I shake my head, and he scowls at me before running back out. My eyes shutter closed and I scrub my forehead.

A wry chuckle comes from Dejan. "Sorry?"

I push to my feet. "Bring your work to your kid's day is overrated. Get back outside while you have a chance."

He claps my shoulder and steps out, avoiding the creaking floorboard like he's always lived here. I take one more breath, and hook my comm in, sending a tap through the frequency to let everyone know I'm back, and step out.

11

REMY

CIERAN'S GOT BEAR DISTRACTED as he shuffles cards. The sergeant sits on the edge of the couch, sword adjusted so he's still ready to jump up at a moment's notice. Blair kneels on the other side of the low table, mesmerized by the flashing cards. I take advantage of his focus, and move past to the kitchen.

Mom's making a cup of tea, and I'm surprised when she turns and hands it to me.

"You okay?" she asks.

I lean against the counter by the sink, tugging the sword belt strapped across my chest so its blade is not digging into the back of my hip. She takes the job of holding up the bar side, smiling softly as I just shrug and tap the side of the mug, bringing the tea down to the perfect sipping temperature.

Mom reaches out and rubs my upper arm, some look falling over her face as she touches chain mail.

"*You* okay?" I lift a wry eyebrow.

"I've just never seen you in full gear outside of pictures before," she says. "Sometimes it's easy to ignore what you really do when you're here and doing normal things."

Something Besim's sister had said a few months back, shaken at the sight of her brother injured in front of her.

"You and all those boys." Mom softly laughs, and I smile. Most of us joined the Army when we were just boys—eighteen, nineteen. Sometimes it's hard to feel young after serving for this long and seeing and doing what we have.

Part of me regrets that she's seeing this side of us.

"But some things haven't changed." A bit of sly humor takes over and I regard her warily. "I thanked Agent Alder for fixing my plants earlier."

My jaw shifts around a rueful smile and I shake my head as she chuckles. "Sorry."

She pats my arm again.

"Where's Dad?" I ask.

"Agent Fortin is getting a lecture about warding plants." We share a laugh. "It's not hard to find out what we do, and she had some questions. I let him take the reins since him unoccupied is about as bad as Bear."

I grin. She's not wrong.

"Do you have a *humuhumu*?"

We both smile at the sight of Bear standing with cards packed haphazardly in his hands, bouncing as Cieran flips a card around.

"This one?"

"Yes!" Bear almost sends cards flying as he grabs it. They're playing with the fish cards, and guarantee he's got at least two matches in his hand that he hasn't figured out yet. Bear's trying to teach Cieran how to say the full *humuhumunukunukuapua'a*, but it's mostly laughing.

Hearing him say the Hawaiian makes some of my guilt come back. I never felt at home on the Islands the way everyone wanted me to. Even after the final trials to get my warlock marks where I passed the tests with a magic dampener on my wrist and fought and navigated with just the clothes on my back and a knife.

I have so many good memories of being there, but it's the memories of the few who didn't welcome me, whose snide comments snuck under my skin and made me always feel a little apart, that have made me not take Bear there yet.

Because he's only a quarter and doesn't have the magma dragon's gift inside, and I can't bear to explain why or watch him be looked at differently. We're still teaching him the language, even if common is used most with me, and some traditions. But maybe it's my own issues getting in the way and I'm robbing him of something.

"Remy." My mother's soft voice centers me back in the kitchen. "Blood doesn't make you belong to somewhere or something." The Hawaiian rushes and ripples and it always feels like the magic in my blood rises to meet the sound. This is something she's told me since I was six and noticed that I was not always the same as my cousins. "Culture and heritage are things to be honored, to be learned. Often we need these things to anchor us, but they do not own us."

She's learned that herself her whole life, sometimes feeling out of place on the Islands or being the "exotic" one in Britannica. But always finding people in both places who didn't care about blood or DNA, just who she was.

"I know," I reply in kind.

She smiles gently. "Then maybe believe it one of these days." It's not judgmental, just a little sad and earnest.

I cover with a sip of tea. It's all a part of me, and I'm a part of the Islands, the raging fire inside tethering me there even if I ever forswear anything to do with my heritage.

Cieran pauses the game and answers his phone, stepping away from the couch. I instinctively lean forward. This team is my place. At least for now.

"Sorry, sir, was in the middle of a pretty intense game of Go Fish." Cieran's reply makes me relax instantly. Just a regular check-in with Wolfe. One he was a minute late for since he was entertaining my kid.

"You're kidding me." Cieran rubs his forehead. "Look, if I see a cop car anywhere near here, I'm slashing tires at the least. They're not blowing this."

I roll my eyes. Great, the update with the Dunhare PD went so well that they must want a patrol in the area. But I agree with Cieran. If Ballagh sees more than she already has, she'll either be in the wind, or more will be caught in the crossfire. I don't even want the Bureau response team here, and would feel a hell of a lot better with just my team and another Drax crew out there instead.

"Whoa, cops?" Dejan's voice breaks in through my ear.

"Sounds like they want a patrol around," I reply, getting a confused look from Mom before she inclines her head in understanding.

Besim grumbles, and Cieran twists to frown at me. We're talking in his ear and Wolfe's in the other.

"Don't worry, Sarge is on it." I smirk a little. "Everyone say hi to CO."

I tilt my head to the side as they don't exactly yell, but it's no whisper either. Cieran doesn't flip me off because Mom and Bear are right there, but he wants to as he hangs up. He does say something in elvish that has Dejan snickering and Besim and I doing the same since we get the jist. Mom's mouth puckers but she smiles behind the frown.

Cieran checks his watch. "Bes, you're up for a break. I'll be out in a second."

I lean forward, wanting to volunteer to go outside instead, take Besim's place on watch. But I get three voices telling me, "Don't even think about it, Rem."

"I hate you all," I grumble.

"I know." Cieran strides over and taps my shoulder with a fist, a question in his eyes. I nod. I'm not really okay, but "okay" is not going to happen until this is all over and probably not for awhile after.

"Cieran, are you coming?" Bear's right behind him.

"Sorry, bud, I gotta go outside, but Bes is coming in and he can finish the game for me."

Bear stomps again, frustration filling up his small body and escaping in a whine.

"Blair," I warn. "Cir has to work."

"I want to *play* with him." Bear glares at me, whole body stiff.

"I will play with you, or Besim can," I say, and Cieran edges a step away.

"NO!" Bear screams and runs off.

A sigh breaks free. That wasn't as bad as it could have been, and I don't blame him because I'm feeling about the same way inside.

"Save yourself." I tap Cieran's shoulder, shaking my head at Mom's unspoken question. I'll go deal with it since I'm the one who upended everyone's lives today.

Alder is nowhere to be seen, and from the voices coming from the office, it sounds like she got roped into the lecture Dad is excitedly giving. Bear's room is the first door in the narrow hallway, separated from mine at the end by the bathroom.

He's figured out how to lock doors, but thankfully didn't this time, and didn't try slamming it shut either. One episode of me unlocking it with an easy spell taught him he's not big enough to lock himself in his room. His low bed is tucked in the corner opposite the door and he sits, back to me, hunched over.

I tap the doorframe and he ignores me. I take a second to silence the two-way setting on the comm, so I can still hear the team, but they can't hear me.

"Bear." I really only use *Blair* when he's in trouble, and he knows. He sniffs and doesn't turn. I take the few steps across the room, picking up some blocks as I go and tossing them into their crate before crouching by the bed.

"What do you feel like?" I ask. It's the question my parents used for me growing up, making it easier for a toddler to express the emotion that was making magic flare up, teaching me the things that would make the magic "glow inside" or "be sleepy."

But Bear makes a stubborn sound and still doesn't turn. Well, proof again that he's my kid.

"I'll go first," I say. "I feel mad that our day got changed and we didn't get to finish at the park. I'm mad that all this is happening today. And I'm a little bit scared."

He peeks over his shoulder. I get that hint of purple in his dark eyes and almost flinch.

"Dad, you are never scared."

I give a small smile. I wish. "Sometimes I am. And it's when I have to protect a lot of people, like you and Grandpa and Grandma."

Bear pivots, still holding his knees up to his chest. "I feel..." His fingers flutter and then clench. "Squiggly inside."

"That's okay. A lot of crazy stuff is happening right now."

He sighs, and legs slide down for him to sit cross-legged. "Why is it happening?"

I swallow hard, and give serious thought to just avoiding it and running away. Good example. Instead, I lean more heavily on my thighs and nearly knock myself off-balance into his bed.

"Because someone I used to know is a bad person, and they want to try to hurt people. We're worried they might try to hurt everyone in this house, so the crew is here to make sure that doesn't happen."

Bear locks on to me and hopefully he didn't hear the slight waver in my voice. He shifts to his knees instead. "Did you get hurted a long time ago?"

My eyes sting for a second. "Yeah."

"You feel squiggly inside." He presses a small hand against my chest.

Mine covers his and I manage to smile again. "Yeah, I do."

He nods like he can actually feel it. Then his brown eyes lock on me with the solemn impending *question* look.

"Dad. What does *shilsa* mean?"

And I laugh—a desperate sound breaking free. He grins back, thankfully with no real understanding. I lean forward to tap my forehead against his.

"Why don't we ask Uncle Dejan?"

Oh, we've done this before and now he really is grinning, an edge of wicked delight there.

I flip the channel back and take the comm out of my ear, turning the volume up and holding it between us to broadcast. "Hey, Dej?"

He acknowledges immediately.

"Bear has a question for you."

"What's up, Bear?"

Bear looks to me for confirmation that he can ask, and I nod. I shouldn't let him repeat the word, but this is what Dejan gets for cursing around a sponge.

"What does *shilsa* mean?"

Laughs echo back, a little tinny through the receiver and Besim's real one booming from the living room in stereo.

"Go ahead, buddy," I say when Dejan doesn't immediately respond.

Dejan huffs and he's at least mentally cursing. "It means you're a silly mammoth head."

Bear dissolves into giggles, his hands covering his mouth not able to contain them all.

"Nice recovery," Besim compliments.

"Thanks," Dejan replies.

"Dad, is it an outlaw word?" Bear recovers enough to ask. About eight months ago I told him we were outlawing "stupid" from the house, and any curse word or word I'm tired of hearing is now an "outlaw" word.

"It definitely is."

"You can't use it until you see a live Vinland mammoth," Dejan says.

"There is one at the zoo." Bear treats the comm to a pitying look.

"Yeah, come on, Dej." Cieran's definitely still snickering.

"The Portal-land zoo has a baby mammoth and it is so cute!" Bear's face scrunches up. He almost melted the day we took the hour drive over to *Portland* for the zoo and saw the few-weeks-old mammoth clomping around.

"I want to tell them about the otters." His hand darts toward the comm, and halts at my raised eyebrow.

"Later. They're working right now."

"How come you're not working?" Low laughs greet Bear's question.

"I am working," I say. "And about to go make sure Besim doesn't eat all the cookies."

"Hey," Besim complains.

Blair grins and leans closer. "Can I have a cookie?"

"Sure." I get ready to say no when he snakes arms around my neck, head tilting to flash his most charming grin.

"And then we can watch cartoons?"

I tap my forehead against his. "No."

He pouts but doesn't give up the hug.

"We never read earlier. Why don't you go get cookies and our book?"

"Yes!" he belts into my ear, and through the comm I'm still holding. He wriggles around me and disappears.

"Sorry," I tell the team. "I might be completely deaf, if that makes you feel better." I catch laughs as I adjust the volume and fix it back in my ear.

"I think we heard that outside," Cieran says. I undo the sword belt around my waist, laying it beside me as I sit with back to the wall.

"I'll mute in a second." I rest my head back, draping arms over knees.

"We don't get to listen?" Dejan asks. "I know you do killer voices."

I chuckle as my thumbs rub along the pads of my fingers, bits of warmth from the friction and from sparking magic bursting under the pattern. "You wish. This mouse is about to kick some serious butt."

"Language," Dejan tuts.

"Mouse?" Cieran's confused. "Wait, those the Everwood books?"

"Yeah. They're all I'd get from libraries for a solid two years."

"My brother loved those." Wistfulness softens Cieran's voice, and a short pang hits me. I'm an only child, and always wanted another sibling. But seeing Cieran who lost a brother as a kid, and then his sister not too long ago, makes me glad in an odd sort of way that I won't have to experience that particular pain.

"Borrow them sometime," I say. "They're still pretty good years later."

"Maybe I will." It sounds more like Cieran's daring himself.

Blair races back in and dumps a lot more than one cookie into my quickly outstretched hands, and a "in my room," reminder has him skidding back into the hall. I stack the cookies atop each other. I'm willing to bet he climbed up the counter and grabbed them all himself, getting some for me too. Either that or Grandma is also allowing all the rules out the window today.

He's back in, holding the book aloft like a trophy, millimeters from smacking me in the face with it as he claims my lap. It takes some shifting and wiggling before we're both settled, and I crack open the book. He hands me a cookie, still not quite understanding how I don't like chocolate even though I carry a bar everywhere. Overdo the magic? Chocolate's the best way to kickstart a recovery and faster regeneration. But it's too sweet for me, and not sweet enough for him.

We did extra chocolate chips in this batch, and I force a bite. It makes my magic jitter a little, responding to whatever it is about chocolate that interacts with magic.

"Okay, I'm out." I mute my comm, and slide the bookmark from the pages. "We'll finish this chapter, okay?"

He nods, already sneaking another cookie, as I start to read.

12

SARA

I EXCUSE MYSELF FROM the warding plant conversation between Fortin and Mr. Kalama. Fortin's ecstatic, thinking she might have finally cracked a case open. I leave my tablet with her, complete with the search I ran to find connections between other cold cases and the information that Keahi gave.

But now it's turning into a "hey, you've been to..." conversation as Mrs. Kalama joins in.

I make my way over to the front window. The street is still innocent and empty except for random cars or pedestrians that don't seem to draw any suspicion from the soldiers. Sergeant O'Donnell is gone, and the half-troll has taken his place.

Besim tracks a slow path from the kitchen to the living room, alternating which viewpoint he has with texting someone important based on the faint smile that creases his face every few messages. I want to ask—he seems the most friendly and approachable—but instead take to the armchair out of his way.

Without my tablet, there's only my notepad and pencil. I'm not confident enough to take a book off the shelf, and besides, I should probably *look* like I'm doing something. Even if that's about to be sketching whatever takes my fancy since there's lot of cozy still-life opportunities in the house.

Blair runs out and there's some muffled scraping and a rattle, and then he zooms back. Besim watches with a grin, and then taps his ear before turning back to the window. A low voice catches my ears, and I angle my ear toward it.

I might not have gotten the elf magic, but I got the enhanced hearing and vision. Even though Remy is in the other room, I can hear him plain as day. Something softens inside realizing he's reading to Blair. And I think I recognize the book. It takes another minute of concentrated listening to confirm.

Yep. It's an Everwood book. I loved those as a kid, and almost bought a copy of one of my favorites—seafaring squirrels fighting pirate rats—last time I was in a bookstore. I start to sketch as Remy reads. They've made it to one of the big battle scenes and the hero mice are about to lose before coming back for an epic victory at the end.

Listening to the story with the comforting *sktch* of my pencil against paper providing a low background noise, takes me back to growing up, when it was just me and my mom and it felt like she cared about me. When we'd curl up next to each other on the couch, a bowl of popcorn between us, each with a book in hand. She'd inevitably stop with her book long before me, then I'd let her take mine and she'd start reading out loud.

I understand why she married my stepdad. I really do. Single mom with a kid and no one to look after me while she worked extra jobs to make sure we could keep the apartment and food on the table? But once she did, it was them and it was me. And then my brother came along, and he was full elf with all the magic, and he definitely got all my stepdad's attention and affection. And then it was just me and my books and high grades because I loved school, and facts and data were always there just waiting to be discovered. I have my birth dad's last name, never fully adopted into the new family.

Blair's, "No, Dad, but they *can't*," has me smiling wistfully as I keep sketching. Augustin the mouse brandishes his sword on my paper, but in the other room, he's just lost and he and his band are on the run.

"Keep listening," Remy reassures.

It makes me want to go apologize to him again for bringing all this right to his door. He's different than the other men, one of whom had a very frosty wife in the room who was not happy to relive the fact that he cheated, and that they have a two-year-old son from it.

Blair's older than that kid, which means that after Remy, she went on and targeted someone else. He hasn't heard that part yet, and probably doesn't need to know because however their relationship ended, it wasn't good.

This house is different than the others too. And it makes me wistful for a past that I never had. Supportive grandparents, a home to live in, a parent who clearly loves their kid. I smudge out a line. I don't need to project my own issues here, but I can still hope for the best for Remy and Blair.

His voice fades in and out as I keep working and try not to attend overmuch to how smooth it is. Hands are hard to draw on a good day, so don't get me started on *paws*. I'm about to erase again and try another set of small lines when I'm aware of a presence peering around the back of the armchair.

Blair gasps and inches closer, not put off when I look at him. "It's our book. Dad, look!"

Remy's suddenly right there, and I can't read anything in his stony expression. I bolt to my feet, clutching at my notepad like I can hide it.

"I'm sorry, I happened to hear you reading." I indicate my pointed ears. "I wasn't trying... I loved those books as a kid," seems to be all I can get out.

Remy's expression doesn't falter and I'm being judged and weighed. I can't miss how he reaches out to Blair like he might be trying to shield him from the agent who was creepily listening in from the other room. Blair tugs on his hand, but the boy's focus is on the notepad.

"Do you have a favorite?" Remy finally asks, and there's still a tenseness that wasn't there moments ago when he was reading.

"*Stormfleet.*" I offer it like a question.

A faint smile emerges, softening his features, and relaxing his shoulders. "That one is good."

Blair starts pulling and twisting around Remy's hand, sensing that his dad's tension is gone.

"Have we read that one, Dad?" he asks.

Remy plants his feet against the pull. "Not yet."

Blair spins and grabs his other hand and starts trying to walk up Remy's legs and hang upside down. Remy's brows lower and he steps back, foiling his son's plans. Undeterred, Blair goes right back for it.

"Can we read it next?"

"We've got to finish this one first." Remy allows the gymnastics and Blair grins at me upside down.

"Can I see your picture again?" he asks.

But I look to Remy for confirmation, and at his nod, I turn the sketch around and present it. Blair flips to slam feet on the ground and releases Remy's hands to come peer at the drawing.

"I will show you my pictures," he announces and barrels off, returning with a sheaf of paper before I can muster another apology to Remy.

Blair spreads his drawings across the low table and beckons to me. After another glance for permission from Remy, I kneel next to Blair.

"These are really good." I'm impressed, and let him tell me all about them. He leans on the table atop crossed arms, alternating bouncing on his knees or sort of kicking his legs out behind him.

"And I colored it blue because that's my favorite."

I nod like I've just been given a high-level academic interpretation of a lopsided fish surrounded by flowers. Sea anemones on second thought. "That was a really good choice. I like the dark blue there." I point to the fins.

He beams back and I'm convinced he's going to look exactly like his dad when he grows up. Not that I've been looking a lot at Remy to make that determination.

I pause, thinking back through that observation. No pointed ears, no vibrant band of color mirroring his fae parent's eye color around his iris, no magic. He looks *human*. And he shouldn't.

I turn to Remy, and his arms cross over his chest, meeting my gaze with that same caution as every other time we've talked. Except for those few seconds after I fixed the plants.

"He doesn't have magic?" I ask softly even though we covered it in the briefing, even though none of the kids have magic and they all should as half-fae. Their fathers all have magic, and Remy's powerful and I just got a brief glimpse of his magic earlier. He didn't cast, but it felt like I'd opened a furnace for those few seconds until he got it under control.

Remy shakes his head. "He should, right?"

I completely understand the doubt in his voice, because I'm suddenly questioning everything I know about genetics and magic. For Blair *not to*, and to not have any fae characteristics…that's getting into genetic modification or selection at a level that's only been theorized because it's wildly unethical.

"Dad has magic," Blair announces.

"I hear it's pretty strong," I say, and immediately wince at the way Remy stills, my brain finally presenting the reminder that he was targeted because of his magic long after my mouth produced the sentence.

"I like when he uses his magic. It makes me feel cozy." Blair tries to balance between table and couch on his hands and knees.

"It what?" Remy stares at him. Unease threatens as I process this statement.

"When you use magic, it makes me warm." Blair kneels on the couch long enough to point at his chest.

Remy and I exchange an uncertain glance.

"Do you use magic around him often?" I ask.

He shakes his head. "Not really, and it's basic stuff like starting a fire." He points to the fireplace. "Cooling a drink off. And I keep some wards around." Remy looks to Blair. "What about when Grandpa uses magic?"

"Cozy!" Blair flops on the couch, arms stretched up to Remy, chuckling over the word.

"He uses it even less than me." Remy locks on to me like I might have some sort of answer.

I'm starting to spin a theory that I already don't like, and he's going to hate. "Could…could you use some now?"

Remy pulls back, and a heavier tread marks Besim coming to join us.

"What do you think that's going to do?" the half-troll asks. It's not antagonistic, but it is questioning, and I understand completely that he will step in to protect Remy if he feels like it's needed, even though Remy with his magic is the strongest person here.

It also seems like there's no secrets among the team. In fact, they're holding some from me, and based on the way they both tap at their ear—Besim once, Remy twice—all this is getting transmitted directly to the others somewhere outside.

"That formula, it wasn't to store magic. Timball kept saying *conduit*, to transmit something through. We already established we think she'd use..." My throat locks up before I can say *kid*, because looking at Blair bouncing on the couch, I can't imagine anyone channeling magic through someone so innocent and destroying a life. Because that's the end result no matter how you look at it.

"Could she be after them both?" Besim asks it calmly but there's a new stillness around him and I don't want to see what he'd be like pissed off.

"That's kinda my question." I really want to apologize, but a soft curse escapes Remy and he sinks down to the couch, automatically shifting his weapons as he does.

"She never lied, but seems like she wasn't always truthful." Raw bitterness snags Remy's voice and he stares at something beyond me.

The look on his face makes me want to give him a hug, but I doubt that'll go over well. He said he knew her for months, much longer than the others, and whatever she did, however she left...it left a gaping wound and it makes me angry. Really angry that he got hurt and she just offloaded Blair because she couldn't be bothered to take care of a kid after who knows what she did to him.

Remy rocks to the side as Blair tackles him in a hug and slams his head against Remy's.

"Ow." But Remy's faint smile returns, and he more gently taps his forehead to Blair's. Remy gets an arm around his son and sets him on the ground in front of him. He glances at me and I'm not sure if he's hoping I'm right or wrong, before a small bit of blue flame appears in his palm.

I'm just as mesmerized as Blair as it wicks and dances. His affinity is wildfire, and even that small bit of magic radiates heat. The small bit of magic I hold is drawn to it as well, recognizing that fire can prepare for new growth even though it might destroy first. His magic is blue, a deep blue, the hottest part of a flame, showing off its strength without him having to cast anything.

"What should I do with it?" Remy asks Blair. The four-year-old would be a hairsbreadth away from it except for Remy's hand on his chest nudging him back.

"Make a firework!"

I follow the quick look Remy gives Besim, and the half-troll dips his chin in response, the burn scarring on his cheek catching the light briefly.

It makes the anger flare at anyone who'd want to hurt or use this man who so clearly cares about his son and his team. And a little at myself for not having more magic or skill to help in whatever fight or confrontation might come with Ballagh.

Remy cups his hands together, masking the flame before his top hand scrapes across his opposite palm and comes away in a closed fist. Blair dances from foot to foot, anticipation bright in his eyes. Remy shakes his head a little, smile flashing, before he flicks his hand open and multi-colored sparks zip and burst into the air, chasing each other and whirling around Blair as he tries to catch them.

A pink spark touches Blair's finger and then bounces off. I reach out my own hand. A green ember floats down and fizzles out against my skin, leaving a faint warmth and tingle. Besim hesitantly lifts his hand to a deep blue one, moving like he's daring himself, and doesn't flinch when it settles against the back of his hand that's suddenly stone grey. The stoneskin fades as the spark disappears, and a quick breath escapes him. Blair tries for an orange one, but it keeps drifting away despite his best efforts.

Remy twists his hand, fingers compressing together, and the remaining sparks group together and settle against Blair's skin like he's some sort of giggling Christmas tree.

One by one, they start to vanish, and I make sure Remy's released the spell. But he hasn't. His fingers still touch, and he watches in muted horror as his son absorbs the magic.

But Blair still laughs, arms outstretched as the magic winks out. "They're tickling under my skin."

Remy's hand flies open, and Blair bounces on his toes. "Do it again, Dad!"

"Maybe later." Remy's voice is hushed. Blair mimics the way Remy held his hand, concentration lining his face like he's about to recreate the charm. And for a moment, we all hold our breath, bracing for him to actually do it even though all evidence says he can't.

And nothing happens. I don't know who is more relieved—me or Remy. If Ballagh had been successful with whatever she'd done to Blair, then he'd be able to absorb magic and spit it back out in a stronger form. A conduit to channel and amplify magic.

"If we saw the final formula, then it looks like he really isn't what she needs." I hate the way it sounds coming out of my mouth. He's not the conduit. "She must be trying to get another kid."

I want to apologize again as Remy's features crease toward nausea again. I can't help but think that any of the other guys we interviewed would be readily volunteering. But maybe *they* weren't what she needed.

"So why target another race?" Besim asks. "Why not another fae?"

I shrug, almost grabbing a marker to cap and uncap as I talk. "I'm not sure. But." I pause to think through it. "The half-fae was really powerful, almost as much as a full. But something didn't work with that. Maybe the human genes limited it somehow? Elves have regenerative magic, so maybe mixing that with fae genes would help with the *mending*."

"What about fire warlock?" Remy asks wryly. I think I get where he's coming from.

"You could probably argue that any of the elements has some regenerative property," I say. "Fire clears, purifies in a way." I hesitate, wincing as I say it. "Or, it could just be her trying again and you being really powerful."

That almost flinch hits him again and he looks away for a moment. Blair jump attacks him for another hug, his little face distorted in a scowl.

"Ow." Remy hisses at the audible snap of discharging static. "You shocked me," he *tsks*.

"Sorry!" his son belts out.

Remy huffs and scoops his son into his lap, not stopping him as Blair starts to poke through the tac vest pockets.

"Can I...?" I hesitate again. Remy and Besim both look at me with a "stop asking if you can ask questions" look.

I clear my throat. Be direct. Something Fortin has been telling me after each interview, but I'm more used to trying to anticipate reactions and therefore, keep the peace.

"Has Blair's doctor said anything about him being…I don't know, different?" I ask.

Remy shakes his head. "I'm not sure I even told her that his…" His jaw clenches, a spasm rocking through his cheek. "That Ballagh is fae."

Besim stands a little closer, reaching out and tapping Remy's shoulder with a fist. Remy glances up at him, then quickly away.

"But she's a general pediatrician, so doesn't really test for any magic or genetics unless there's concerns." And the way Remy's mouth clamps again, he hasn't been raising concerns in either department. None of the other kids had flags either, but maybe we needed to dive into their medical records a little.

Besim clears his throat softly, and Remy follows his smile and arched brow back to where Blair has opened a vest pocket and is pulling out chocolate bars.

"Bear," Remy reprimands gently and replaces the bars. Blair flashes a sunnily innocent smile back up at him.

"Can you make another firework?" He slides off Remy's lap.

Remy gently rebuffs the request. "Let's pick something else to do."

Blair's shoulders crumple for a brief moment, then he turns bright eyes up at me. "Can we color again?"

I can't help but smile back, an expression that feels warmer than it has been in a long time, creating a lightness inside to match. I love kids and these days don't get to interact with many. Most of the other agents I'm friends with are like me—too committed to jobs for family, and I'm not sure that I'd be rushing to hang out with any niece or nephew my brother might give me.

"Bear." Remy's voice breaks my attention, and the warlock shakes his head.

"I don't mind if it's okay with you," I tell him, and almost feel shy at the look he gives me. Evaluating in a different way than before, but like the other times, I'm not sure what he's seeing.

"Okay," he finally says. Blair's quick to get coloring books and a box of crayons and assigns me a page in a storybook.

"You can tell him no," Remy says quietly, faint humor in his eyes showing the resemblance between the two of them.

I smile as I get comfortable on the floor. "It's okay. Coloring's a lot more fun than waiting around."

Wry agreement quirks his mouth, and I almost ask if he wants to color with us before clamping my lips shut. I'm already not being very professional by coloring a scene from a cartoon to begin with, I don't need to cross another personal and professional boundary by asking Specialist Kalama to join us.

He moves off before I can make anything awkward or apologize for what I was thinking. I hyperfocus on filling in the puffy trees until the feeling passes.

Fortin reappears and just gives a flat-lipped smile but doesn't correct. I know she sees how hard this is for Blair, but I might get a pointed comment later about how analysts, and definitely field agents, don't get this comfortable on assignment.

But it's keeping him content and occupied, and it's fun to trade books so I can color a dinosaur next. I make it purple, my favorite.

Remy sets a reusable water bottle covered in stickers next to Blair and places a water glass on a coaster next to me.

"Thanks." I glance up, offering a smile. He doesn't seem as guarded as before, and inclines his head.

"Do you—" He cuts off and strides to the window, heat trailing in his wake.

Besim looms over us, a smile that's a little too cheery on his face. "Bear, let's go check in with your grandparents for a second."

Fortin strides over, a comm in her ear that links her to our team outside. She hovers by the front door. Blair's protesting, and I'm frozen to the ground. *What's happening?*

"Agent!" Fortin snaps and I whip my wide-eyed gaze to her. "Get him back to the office."

But Besim's already picking Blair up, walking him over to Mr. Kalama who's appeared in the office doorway, looking about as frantic as I feel. He takes Blair and Besim strides back past me where I'm still locked in place.

"I see them," Remy says, watching through a crack in the blinds. "Purple eyes?"

He must get an affirmative, since he curses in what's probably Hawaiian.

"Dad?" Confusion and some fear tremors through Blair's voice. Remy turns only to point at the office. His father wordlessly obeys, and they disappear.

"Will the wards hold them?" Besim asks, setting next to the front door. Fortin falls back closer to me as I finally get to my feet.

"Should. I'm going to strengthen them now," Remy replies. "Let me know when they dive again."

"Magpies," Fortin tells me, like that'll explain everything. "Ballagh's probing."

My fist shakes around a crayon. I can't remember what I'm supposed to do. Five feet away, Remy extends his arm, hand scooping, before he taps a fist to his chest. There's another ripple of heat. Besim stays alert by the door, moving only to glance through the thin crack in the curtains.

"All three?" Remy clarifies. He starts to move to the door, but Besim blocks his way. A frustrated sound rips from Remy, a much deeper version of his son's. "I can do this better outside."

He doesn't like whatever answer he gets since he shoots a glare at Besim who wordlessly raises a shoulder. And doesn't move.

Fortin lowers her hands and the chill surrounding her fades. Some frost fades from my glass. "All three birds are dead," she says.

I don't know if I'm supposed to acknowledge that or not. I'm supposed to be backup, supposed to be at least guarding the office door. Supposed to be holding a knife instead of a coloring implement.

"Sara." Fortin's low voice jerks my attention to her. Patience is the expression she's presenting, but I feel like there's some disappointment not far beneath. Which brings back some uncomfortable, and familiar, emotions that I'm used to feeling around my family.

"I..."

"Go let them know it's all clear." She gestures to the office. I don't dare to look at Remy or Besim as I obey, gingerly setting down the crayon before I do.

Rebecca has Blair in her lap, letting him flip the pages of a book. She's too busy watching the door and her husband. Keahi is braced at the entrance, slowly relaxing as I force a smile and give a wavering, "All good."

Blair shoves the book away and scrambles over to peer around me. "Dad?"

I step away as boots stride over and Remy appears in my periphery. "All good, Bear."

"What happened?"

"Remember when birds were trying to eat Grandma's plants?" Remy asks.

Blair grins. "And you scared them with popping magic?"

Remy ruffles his hair. "Yeah. Just something like that."

The kid looks back to me. "Can we color again?"

I swallow hard, forcing a look at Remy. But he doesn't seem disappointed. Yet. Maybe he and his teammate were too busy to notice me freezing. He just inclines his head. He's okay with us coloring.

"Sure." My voice isn't completely steady, but Blair doesn't notice, just scampering back to the coffee table.

"You good?" Remy's question halts me. I force a smile and nod and escape.

For a few minutes, it was like I'd forgotten that Maeve Ballagh was a real and present threat. Now, with the unpleasant reminder that she's coming, and coming soon, I don't know if I'm going to be able to do anything to help stop her.

13

REMY

NIGHT IS FALLING FAST, and the churning unease has only gotten louder. Dej and Besim are outside, ghosts in the growing darkness. Three other agents are out there too, dressed in black fatigues and with short swords that look like standard government issue.

Agents Fortin and Alder are updating their headquarters. Comms are quiet except for the periodic tapping started off by Cieran, and echoed back by us as check-ins. Nothing has stirred since the magpies earlier. It wasn't much of an attack, just a reminder that she's out there. There were a few more sightings through the day, but always from a distance.

Blair needs to be getting ready for bed, especially since his normal nap time got skipped. But I'm not about to leave him in the room off the side of the house, even with all the extra wards I put up earlier today. He's curled up on the couch, head on my leg, soft blanket covering him. He hasn't been poking at the knife belt by his face for at least ten minutes, so he's fallen asleep.

My hand rests protectively on his head, fingers alternating between brushing his hair and tracing a protective ward.

Cieran's in the kitchen, third cup of coffee in hand, leaning against the counter, politely listening to my dad ramble on about his newest research endeavor. But I can see Cieran's eyes glazing over from here.

I take pity on my sergeant.

"Hey, Dad," I softly call. His attention immediately homes on me. "Watch Bear for a minute? My leg's falling asleep."

He sets his mug down, and comes over as I ease out from under Blair. He curls further under the blanket, but doesn't wake as Dad settles in. I shake out my leg on the way into the kitchen.

Cieran shifts around the counter to lean on his forearms. I take out a new mug and start making myself some tea.

"Thanks for the rescue," he laughs softly.

I turn against the counter as my tea steeps. "You were looking a little lost."

"That obvious?"

"Just space out your nods and 'reallys?' a little more and he definitely won't notice." I bob the tea bag, watching the color deepen.

Cieran chuckles, and spins his mug around. "Doing okay?" he asks.

"Would you be?"

"Hell no."

My eyebrow arches and he concedes with a tilt of his head before returning to spinning the mug. "How's Bear?"

I check again, even though it's only been a few minutes. "He's hanging in there. I'm surprised we only had the one meltdown today."

Movement draws my gaze to Agent Alder. She smiles at my dad and takes a seat in the armchair. I've got a view of her face and there's a weird shift inside me as she successfully draws my dad into soft conversation.

Watching her earlier with Blair had been...different. She didn't have to sit there coloring for over an hour with him, but she did. And I think she was part of the reason Blair calmed down for so long.

She looks a lot steadier now than she did earlier with the magpies. I guess I can't really judge if this is her first time in the field. Fates know how jittery I was on my first deployment.

"She's not bad as far as agents go," Cieran says. I flick a glance at him. He lifts a shoulder, but I've also been staring at her, telling myself I've got an excuse for watching her every move. I'll be glad when they're all out of the house and things can go back to normal.

He seems to be expecting something back from me, but a quick burst of static prefaces Besim's low voice. "Got movement."

We abandon mugs, and pull towards the living room. Alder sits up tall, locked on to us.

"Talk to me." Cieran taps his sword hilt. I reach back over my shoulder and check the release on my basalt blade.

"Not sure, but there's some shadows around that are being dodgy."

"I see it too," Dejan breaks in.

Cieran nods to my dad and he scoops up Blair and retreats into the smaller, window-free study. Alder comes over to us, hands clutching at each other.

"Where?" one of the other team breaks in.

I can practically hear Besim and Dejan rolling their eyes before Besim replies. "Third streetlamp down."

"What do I do?" Alder asks me. I'm trying to listen to Cieran and the others, but she's a little pale and fidgety.

"You know how to use that?" I point to her knife.

"Um...I'm trained in basic combat skills."

Great.

"Hang back by the office. *If* anything gets through, you'll need to be ready to use it."

"Okay." She nods, but her hands clasp and her attention darts to the front door.

Fortin appears and taps her arm. They fall back to the office, and at least Fortin carries a short sword with confidence.

We head for the front door. Cieran twitches the window curtain back, glancing out. I press a hand to the door, closing my eyes, reaching out and testing the wards I've placed around the fence, the house, and the back gardens. The wards I doubled-up around the front door pulse back brighter.

"Check in," Cieran murmurs.

No other movement is reported, but unease scrapes along my arms and digs into my nerves.

"Magpie," Besim's voice surges up, and we tense.

"Remy!" a voice calls and I press my forehead against the door, trying to shake the way it worms into me. This time her words aren't coarsened by a magpie's beak. It's her. Cieran grabs my shoulder.

"Can we at least have a civil conversation?"

I'm glad of his hold, because it feels like I'm going to split between desire and revulsion.

"Am I just shooting this *crytch*?" Dejan asks.

"Hold," Cieran says. "Let's try not to bring a war to the neighborhood."

I shake my head in response to Cieran's look. Opening the door will weaken some of the wards, and I'm not going to be able to talk to her face-to-face.

"I know you're in there." Her voice lilts singsong. "And I know about your friends standing watch out here. It's cute." I can almost see the way she checks her nails when slightly irritated. "Making friends with the agents?"

I flex my fingers, the comforting heat of fire building in my palm. Something I can actually control.

"Hopefully they haven't totally turned your head with stories. This could be just a business arrangement, Remy."

Well, that sounds horrifying.

Her huff is audible even through the door. Cieran keeps one eye on me and the other on her through the window. I don't want to know what she looks like. I don't want to know where she is. My hands shake and the sharp scent of fire grows around me.

"Easy, Rem," Cieran says.

"She's calling magic." Dejan's voice sharpens. A rumble cuts through a second later, and I wince. She's busted through the fence wards.

"*Fir*. Nightmares," Dej reports.

"What?" Panic fills another agent's voice before an unholy shriek fills the air.

The door shudders and my warding spells glow gold around the frame. Cieran and I take a step back, drawing weapons.

The ring of steel announces the two agents behind us getting ready. Another shudder and a startled cry filled with fear and "Dad?" nearly splits my heart in two. Blair's awake.

And I can't go help him. It doesn't stop me turning like I can reassure him. Alder is all I see, and she grips her knife with a little more confidence, giving me a nod like she's ready to stab the first thing she sees.

"One down," Besim breathlessly reports. "I'm headed around."

Cieran tilts his head side-to-side and taps the band on his wrist. A shield whirls out, the edges latching together to form a rounded buckler.

"Clocking three more." Dejan's report is strained. "Arrows aren't doing shit. I'm coming down."

"Ready?" Cieran asks.

Not really, but I nod. Flames curl around my left hand, and the other draws my basalt sword. The grip is wrapped in treated leather to resist most of my flame. It settles against my palm, trying to ground me.

Cieran releases the shield grip and uses his hand to grab the door handle. One glance back, one nod from me, and he throws open the door, stepping in front of me, shield up and sword ready. I come behind, attack spell releasing as soon as I see her standing in the front gate.

We're halfway to the gate when darkness rises to my left in equine form, red eyes and snorting flames. Terror tries to snare my heart. It rears up, front hooves flaming until Cieran whirls to the side, striking up at its exposed chest.

It pivots away with unearthly speed. Then comes right back, lashing out with hooves, spitting sparks at him.

Maeve raises her hand, and for a second I just stare. Her dark hair is still tinged purple, the same color that glows in her irises as she summons magic. Fitted jeans, heeled boots, and tank top shows muscled arms.

I slam a hand up, blocking her buffeting casts, but my boots still scrape back against the walkway.

She's got a full fae's features: refined, high cheekbones, luminous eyes, sharp smile. Cunning lurking in every curve.

"Just who I wanted." She strides forward, stepping over another ward like it's nothing. My heart gives a little. "Don't try to be a hero, Rem."

"It's not happening." I spin my basalt blade as I call up another attack blast and use the basalt to amplify the casting. Fire spews from the blade and ripples across the walkway towards her feet. She waves her hand and it parts.

"I forgot how tantalizing your magic is." She bats eyes at me.

I don't have a reply, because she's forced me back a step again. But her attention is on me, and not on the dark shape stealthing behind her.

Dejan swings his knife, but she snaps her fingers and he's halted mid-strike. Something twists up her face—anger, malice. I was only ever too young and dumb to see it past the smiles.

Cieran is back at my side, sword dripping with smoky black. Dejan is getting progressively more pissed that he can't move. Then Maeve slowly smiles.

A scream erupts from the house. I twist, all training forgotten, my heart compressing at the sound of Blair's distress. Then something yanks me backward, and I go flying, hitting the street. I barely manage something to cushion the fall, but a grunt shows Cieran stunned a few feet away.

I crane my head up to see Maeve stalking toward me. Dejan fights off a towering figure and Besim is barely hanging on as two more nightmares circle up around him.

Maeve extends a hand to me. I twist, scrambling to my feet and throwing a bolt of uncontained fire magic at her. Vibrant blue light floods the street, a rumble following. She shouts something and as she dispels it, I throw a knife.

She's too distracted to see. It hits her leg, and she staggers, face slack in shock. Darkness swoops down, and a winged nightmare catches her before she falls, avoiding another bolt of magic. I'm tossed backward again by whatever she did the first time, thrown out of reach as her mount takes to the skies.

Another scream comes from the house. My world freezes as a wolf-like creature races from the front door with Blair in its oversized jaws. Something bolts after, landing on the wolf before it starts to spin out into smoke.

Agent Alder.

And I'm helpless as the creature phases out, taking the agent and my son with it.

14

SARA

OH CRAP.

I don't know what I'm thinking.

Two shadow wolves break in through the front door. One mauls Fortin's leg despite her sword and frigid magic. Dodges a blast from Keahi. The other shadowy shape launches and pins Keahi to the wall. I muster courage from somewhere and stab it with shaking knife. Smoke bleeds from its side and it spins, bulky head hitting me and throwing me to the ground for my trouble. My shoulder takes the brunt of my fall, the impact stealing my breath.

It happens in slow motion, the wolf stalking toward Rebecca. Biting her as she tries to shield a sobbing Blair. It grabs him and runs.

No.

I follow. Sprinting. Racing. Not going to look Remy in the eye and tell him I lost his son.

I tackle the damn thing. Feel it shift. And the world goes black.

15

REMY

I STARE AT THE spot in the star-speckled sky where they disappeared. Ignoring the bursts of activity. The neighbors coming to see what the hell happened. Why two Drax Guard are lying in the street. Calls for *medic!*

Something pounds through me, and I don't dare give it a name. He's gone. What does my life look like if I don't go after him?

Cieran's hands fall on my shoulders. I stare at him. His lips move, blood streaks down his neck, and his hat is missing.

He's gone. *Blair's gone.*

Cieran shakes me, and coherence rushes back as my neck snaps back. "Remy!"

Then it hits me. Hits me so hard I can't breathe. Punches through my heart and scores my gut so all I can manage is a whisper. "He's gone. She took him."

"I know, Rem. I know." He gently interrupts my repeated words. "Get up."

My hands curl around his arms and he heaves me to my feet.

"You good?" He looks me over like he's not the one bleeding.

"Bear..."

"I know. We'll get him back." He scoops up his hat from the pavement, and jams it back on with a curse.

All I can do is follow as he limps back to the house, the door torn wide open. The gardens and grass are trampled, burned spots scattered around in the shape of hooves. Besim hurtles over, and Cieran barely dodges his grab, and I just sort of take one of his rib-crushing hugs.

"Where's Dejan?" Cieran asks as I numbly stagger back a step from Besim.

"Inside with the other medic."

Inside. The word fills me with panic. The shadows were inside the house. Mom. Dad.

I push past Cieran before they can stop me, or go first. The armchair is overturned. An agent in black fatigues sprawls on the wood floor, and he's not getting back up. I track more blood around to where Dejan bandages a very pale Fortin's leg.

"Where's Sara?" she rasps at me. I stare back, wanting to shake her because Bear is gone and they didn't do enough. But...

Neither did I.

"They took her and Blair." It takes a second to register that the raspy voice is mine.

She braces hands against the floor, head tipping back against the wall, wincing as Dejan puts more pressure on and ties off the bandages. "Shit."

"Remy?" Dad's voice breaks through. He stands in the office doorway, hunched over a little. And horror spreads across his face at the sight of my empty hands. "Blair?"

"Gone." I'm one second from snapping and I don't know if it's going to be tears or fire when I do.

He sags further against the frame. "I'm sorry, Rem. I tried. I..."

A gentle sound jerks both of our attention and I push into the office after him. Mom is on the ground amidst scattered papers and books, another agent wrapping her arm. She sees me and tries to get up, needing Dad's help to get there.

"Are you both okay?" My voice is still coming eerily distant.

Mom nods, but reaches out to me, worry and apology there. I back away, pushing past more figures who are coming in, Bureau badges winking in the lights. Cieran talks to someone on his phone and another agent in front of him while Dejan dabs at the back of his head.

I get three steps out into the yard before my knees buckle, sending me to the ground. My hands curl against my legs splayed out in front of me. Lights flash blue and white—police rushing in too late and getting pulled into setting a perimeter. An ambulance wails up.

Besim drops into a crouch beside me. Dejan joins a moment later, balancing his bow across his knees.

Besim's hand clasps my shoulder. "We'll get him back."

There's absolutely no other option they're considering right now. I don't have a response. Not until Cieran comes to stand in front of us.

"Just got off with Wolfe. This is now a rescue mission and we have full lead. Remy, your parents are going to the hospital to get checked out. Go with them—"

"She took *my son*." My voice lashes out, magic flaring with it.

"I know," Cieran returns evenly. "And you know protocol."

He doesn't flinch before my barely contained fury. I do know protocol. Usually if there's heavy emotional attachment, that person is off the team, the mission, whatever. But I'm not letting them, or another crew go get my son without me. Not letting someone else face off with *her*.

"I'm going."

Dejan and Besim both reach out to tap my leg. They aren't mad at Cieran for bringing it up. They know it too. But they have my back and they'll make sure I don't do anything stupid. Or will be right there doing it with me. And when I look back at Cieran, I see the exact same thing in his eyes.

"Okay," he says. "What do you need?"

I can track almost anything with a spell, can track without magic too, but they left no trace, so magic it is. And all I'd need is something of Bear's, or Maeve's.

Bad news for her—Bear shares blood with both of us, and all it's going to take is a drop of mine fed into a tracker spell. Because we all know that she's not letting him go until she has me.

"To get him back," I reply, jaw clenched.

Cieran extends a hand down and I grab it. Once on my feet, surrounded by my crew, and their *pissed off* faces, I settle back into myself. "Just need to spin a tracker."

Cieran nods. "Do your thing, Rem, and get us a direction. We'll grab any extra gear we have. We'll get them."

And there's nothing but certainty there. Certainty I try to hold as we go back inside. The agents and police part and Dad pushes forward, halting as I don't look at him. Just pull a knife and prick my left index finger. I call up magic into the palm of my right hand. It's too bright, too hot, responding instantly to the chaos inside.

I take a deep breath. I need calm and steadiness to regulate the spell so it can stretch as far as it needs to find Bear and not drain me in the process. It's about control, boundaries, regulating the power output with words and physical motion.

My hand clenches, extinguishing the fire for a moment before I call it back, much smaller and controlled. Warm and inviting. *Cozy*. Bear's descriptor echoes back and nearly undoes all the work.

"Take your time." Cieran's murmur steadies me.

I set the parameters with short words in Hawaiian—*search, find*—the magic sparking and popping before it settles out into a wavering outline of a compass. *Blair.* I squeeze a drop of blood into the middle of it and the translucent needle spins. Already searching and picking up traces of him everywhere in the house.

I step outside, cup hands and give it the last instructions before tying it back to me like a thread only I can see or feel. My hands flick apart and the spell scatters, racing away. I close my eyes, inhaling. The tracker spreads across the city, over the countryside, stretching into several other cities.

But nothing.

Nothing.

Until a faint pulse picks up in the back of my head. My eyes snap open. It's fifty miles away, high up in the Cascade Mountains marching their way through the state.

I turn to Cieran. "Are there any grif squads on duty tonight?"

"Squad Ten," is the immediate answer.

"Map."

He pulls out his map and notebook from his leg pocket. A snap of my fingers brings better light above it. I listen for the tracking spell again, then flip a few pages until I get the mountains.

"Here. Or around here." I point to a remote spot in the middle of the range.

Cieran nods. "Okay, we can get dropped in and then hike in the rest of the way. I'd rather she didn't see us coming."

He makes a call and ten minutes later, we're back out with packs over shoulders and canteens filled as the griffin shifters of Squad Ten land on the road. Only the squad lead shifts back to human form as we reach their side—we can't communicate otherwise.

Cieran gives the quick brief and shows Sergeant Beck the location I've pinpointed. The nearly seven-foot shifter turns to me. The grif squad's tan fatigues stretch over his bulky frame, and he's got knives strapped everywhere just in case his two-ton griffin form can't get the job done if he's attacked.

"Someone's got your kid?" he asks, voice deep and eyes glinting in the light of the streetlights.

"Yeah." I'm still hovering between frozen and explosively angry. A ripple runs through the three other griffins lying or crouched on the street. One snaps wings, and beaks clack all around. A uniformed officer steps back, hand falling to short sword.

Dejan rolls his eyes. We're used to the griffin shifters, fought alongside them multiple times before and after they've dropped us in for missions.

"You need backup?" Beck asks Cieran.

Our sergeant offers a mirthless smile. "Might once we get up there and scout it out. She's got nightmares at least."

One of his team, a tawny gold with blazing red wings hisses, tail lashing, and Beck glances his way. Griffins are able to mindspeak to each other in and out of shifted forms. Looks like they've had a run-in with nightmares before and it wasn't good.

"All right. Get on and hang on. We'll get you there quick as we can." He gives me a nod and turns on his heel, effortlessly taking griffin form, a more muted lion body with scars tracing down his left side, and a coppery sheen to his wings.

This is going to be one hell of a story spreading around the city and told in the neighborhood for years. We each take a griffin, and I climb on, settling hands in the harness at the base of the griffin's wings, lying flat on my stomach along his back.

A sharp chirp, and they're moving, racing several steps for momentum before launching into the air, gaining altitude, until another signal allows me to sit up straight. We speed east through wisps of cloud and scattered moonlight.

Hang on, Bear. I'm coming.

16

Sara

Brightness bursts in and I sprawl on the ground. It takes a second for the shock to wear off and Blair's screams to filter in. The sound rebounds off stone, echoing back on itself. The shadow wolf prowls in and out of the light from the flickering lightbulb dangling from the ceiling, ears back in annoyance at the sound. I scramble over, scooping the kid into my arms and pressing us both against the nearest wall.

"It's okay, Blair, it's okay!"

He latches on to me, sobbing. "Where's Dad? *I want Dad!*"

"Ugh." A feminine voice announces the owner of heeled boots clicking across the floor. "What's this?" She frowns down at me then turns to the shadow wolf. "I just wanted the kid, not some agent. One job."

She shakes her head, flicking fingers, and the wolf slinks off to the nearest dark corner to merge with the shadows.

"Who are you?" She crouches easily in the heels, fingers with long nails pressing together. I shield Blair more with my body.

"I'm not going to hurt the kid." She rolls her eyes. "Honestly, everyone got the wrong impression. I just want Remy. Is that *so* hard?" She pushes up, wincing and cursing as she presses a hand glowing with magic to her leg. At least someone got a hit in.

I swallow, licking parched lips. Blair stops crying, audibly at least, but doesn't let go.

"Maeve Ballagh?" I ask.

She twists back to me, performing a little bow with hands flicked out to the side. "Present." She saunters back over. This lady doesn't skip the gym, and she looks like she could probably chuck me across the room on pure strength alone. "And you are?"

"Agent Alder."

The shattering of the Courts broke the power full fae could hold over a name, but it's still best practice to *not* give them the chance to try. Especially one who just kidnapped you.

She squats again. "Hmm. I've met my fair share of agents. Don't take this the wrong way, girlfriend, but...you're a little scrawny for one."

I pull back a little. How is that not offensive?

A grin swerves across her face. "But I guess you probably have the same moral uprightness, so a grand speech attempting to convince you to come on over to my side because someone with a sense of snark would be *so refreshing* around here"—she glares at a dark corner—"probably won't work?"

I sniff, making sure my hold on Blair is still solid. "I don't generally hang out with traffickers."

She laughs. "Boring, aren't they?"

And a host of other immoral and illegal things, but *boring* is clearly the worst crime.

I jolt as her finger pokes my arm. "Relax," she chides. "I just want to know if you have magic." She flicks a loose bit of hair away from my ear. "What, half-elf?"

I twist my head away. Sometimes I try to pass as human with only a little silver in my green eyes and reddish hair not starkly Slavic blonde, but my ears end up giving me away. She snaps her fingers and a sort of buzzing runs all over me. I squirm, trying to get away from it, and another muffled sob comes from Blair.

"No tracker." Maeve stands. "You know anything about the Drax soldiers?"

"Nothing except you probably really pissed them off." I am assuming they will be tearing apart the world to find Bear and I can probably hitch a ride back with them.

"Oh, I hope so. Remy stabbed my leg, which was really rude considering our history. But he's attached to that one for whatever reason." She rolls her eyes in Blair's direction.

"Is he not your kid, too?"

"I guess." She reaches up and swats at the dangling lightbulb. It steadies and glows a little brighter. "But he's not especially useful to me. He's probably only really useful to Remy."

I stare open-mouthed at her as she swings over to a table in the corner and begins sifting through several stacks of papers. With more light, I can see over to some passageways cutting away through the heavy rock ceiling. Musty smell, lack of windows and natural light, and knobbled rock above. I'm willing to bet we're underground somewhere.

Great. She's got a lair.

"Then why'd you take him? You said he wasn't what you needed," I say. "He's not a conduit."

She swivels around, one perfectly shaped brow rising. "Oh, the nerds figured out the papers I had to leave behind?"

There's really no point in denying when I've already said it. Her light laugh makes the bulb brighten again and she leans against the table.

"I figured Remy would make things difficult, so the kid here is leverage in case I couldn't get Remy. Honestly." She rolls her eyes. "And they'll know it. Remy's smart. Too smart sometimes."

Blair shifts a little. "Where's Dad?" His whisper is clogged with tears.

"I don't know. But I'm sure he's coming." That's about all I can give him.

"I want him."

"Me too," Maeve cuts in. "I want to try again. I think I have a better handle on what I need this time." She's standing over us again.

"What do you mean?" I stare up at her.

"If I could get pregnant without a guy, I'd do it. Oh, there's clinics." She waves her hand. "But the process is too unpredictable and you can't be sure of what you're really getting. Plus the paper trail." It's said with a little smirk and head toss like that's a funny inconvenience. "Although Remy needed some extra persuasion, he's the closest I've gotten."

Her words sink in. Remy's reactions.

"What did you do?" I whisper in horror.

She rolls her eyes. "Nothing more than he might have done if our positions were reversed."

"He wouldn't." My voice is still hushed. "He's a good guy." I've only known him for *hours* but I feel certain of this.

"Aw." She clasps her hands together. "Does someone have a crush?"

I narrow my eyes. Honestly she should have stuck to the whole sultry, powerful villain thing, because now I'm wanting to actually use the knife I don't have anymore because I lost it when I tackled a nightmare.

She leans closer. "Hate to break it to you, but he's probably not going to reciprocate. I keep an eye on all the attempts, and he's a little skittish around women. Which." She props a hand on her hip, acting like she's thinking. "Maybe that's my bad?"

Some unintelligible sound breaks from me, jumbled in my anger. "*Why* are you doing this? You think you can bring back the Courts? You're insane!"

Maeve laughs, not even put off by my outburst. Blair still clings to me and I'm not letting him go. I owe Remy that at least.

"Insane, genius." She waves her hands like she's weighing each word. "I'm using cutting edge genetic modification that lab nerds are only *dreaming* of. And it's going to work. But you wouldn't know anything about that, would you? No magic, no real power, you look like you're more used to hiding behind something than taking charge."

That one lands, and she knows it based on her smirk.

"Come on," she *tsks*. "You've never wanted more magic, more power? Never wanted to make changes with the snap of your fingers?" Maeve glances down at me, some pity there. "Maybe not, huh?"

All I can do is glare back.

"It was better days with the Courts. Near immortality, the most powerful casters in the world, unlimited shapechanging and glamour, no boundaries on magic. Now it's four hundred years of life, fractions of power, basic glamour, and all these rules on what we can and can't do."

"You ever think the Courts were broken for a reason?" I snap. From what the history books say, there were plenty of elves, shifters, and humans fighting against the domineering fae through their reigns in the Early and Middle Centuries. "Who do you think's going to let you do this?"

"Let me? Girl, I've got enough interested parties to keep me protected while I do this. And once I succeed and sit on the high throne..." She shrugs. "All fae will have to obey the queen again." Ballagh's lip curls in a smile. That's the part that she's going to enjoy the most.

"You could help out. I could use an agent on my side, keep me updated on some things. Maybe even figure out a way to get you more magic. That pesky human side has you too limited." She sidles closer and I put my shoulder more firmly between us. She just laughs lightly.

"I'd keep Remy around. Maybe you two could uh..." Her eyebrows lift suggestively. "Once I get what I need, obviously. His genetics and magic are just..." An appreciative noise breaks from her, and revulsion heaves in my stomach. Blair huddles closer.

"You're sick," I whisper.

The sneering anger slides back across her refined features. "Honestly, hon, don't you get out in the world? It's a freaking mess and the only way to stay on top is to just take what you want."

I have no reply, my mouth hanging open as I stare at her.

She rolls her eyes again. "Yeah, okay. I definitely don't need you around, because this flabbergasted thing every few seconds is gonna get real old, real fast. I don't need an agent anyway, just the kid. Remy will do anything once I dangle—what's his name?" The smirk returns and I really want to punch her.

"So I'll take him." Her fingers curl and some invisible force pulls on Blair. I try to hang on, and he grips my shirt with supernatural strength, but we're slowly being separated. He's crying, reaching out, flailing midair. I try to get to him, but it's like running into a wall. I scream and punch the air, gaining a fraction of an inch. I'm not going to let Blair, or Remy, get used like this.

The emotion boiling inside lends my scraps of magic more strength and I hurl as much as I can at her. It's mere sparks, an inconvenience compared to what she has, but it slaps across her face leaving little streaks like ash. Maeve pauses with a murderous look.

But even with the distraction she hasn't let Blair go. I strain again, but I'm running into a super-charged wall.

"Take out the trash, will you?" She tilts a look over her shoulder and the wolf prowls from the shadows.

I'm about to start screaming in terror as it comes toward me, flames licking its jaws and sparking in its eyes. Another shadow looms behind it—a horse with red eyes, growing bigger and bigger with every heartbeat.

Maeve strides away, pulling a weeping Blair with her. I push up against the rock wall, bracing myself, then lunge forward, trying to make it down the hallway after them, but the horse blocks my path. The wolf's paws drop on my shoulders, and I'm knocked down with a shout. My fists phase through, and the sparks of my magic wink out against the midnight dark coats.

Teeth latch into my shirt and I'm being dragged down a different hallway, the horse stomping after us, its smoke smothering my cries and struggles.

Rough cement digs at my hands and exposed skin above my belt, and my shirt rips at the shoulder. Then a burst of fresh air shimmies through the horse and the wolf releases me. I roll, scrambling away, but they just look at me with heads tilted and shadows dripping in the moonlight. Even the horse has a predatory stalk.

I stumble back. Nightmares feed off fear and if they have teeth in you when you finally die from a terror-induced heart attack, you'll fade into shadows like them. Live a half-life where you crave fear-filled souls. It sounds great.

A cloud darts over the moon and all I'm left with are flaming eyes coming closer and closer. I wish I can say I don't whimper, but it's something really close to that before I turn and *run.*

Shrieks echo into the night. I stagger downhill, barely enough light to avoid crashing into trees or being taken out by low-hanging bushes. A guttural bellow rises, and I trip over a log, rolling and tumbling downhill before I finally slide to a halt and get back to my feet.

The woods are silent. I spin in a circle. Somehow we'd gotten to the mountains, and I'm halfway up the side of one. No sign of the nightmares, but they'll be thriving in the dark. The moonlight slithering through branches gives plenty of shifting shadows for them to work with.

A breath rasps from me and I pat my pockets. With the breaking of the Courts and the passing centuries since decreasing their power, fae have become much less susceptible to things like iron and salt. It can still sting, especially against more powerful ones, but you're honestly better off with magic or weapon in hand if they decide to be evil manipulative *crytches.*

But fae-created creatures like nightmares still are affected, since they were created well before the shattering and somehow stuck around. Of course, I don't have any iron on me. It's long lost in the woods. My knife is back at Remy's house. Not like I really know how to use it anyway.

Think, think, *think!*

I snap my fingers and something snorts in response. Red eyes gleam three paces away and I take off again, stumbling and tripping,

Water. I've got to find running water. Get across a river which will give me enough time to cross some branches.

Pain digs into my side with each stride, and panting breaths rip through my lungs after a minute. I've never been much of a runner, and either these things are also terrible runners or they're toying with me.

It takes another few minutes, and at least two slender branches whipping across my face, before running water sounds over my thrashing. I limp onward, a sound of relief breaking.

And then my world flips upside down.

Triumph shrieks and I roll away from flailing hooves. Teeth latch on to my boot and I scream, trying to get to the river through scattering sparks. I drag myself forward as something hauls back on my leg. Heaviness settles on my shoulder, the grip of teeth trying to make it through the bare defense of my ragged shirt. My heart rams against my chest, but I'm not ready to lie down and die yet.

Cold splashes over my hands and then I'm face-first in the river. A panicked howl sounds, and the tension on my boot releases. This river is deep and I'm barely keeping my head above water, trying to get to the other side. When I finally make it, flopping and gasping like an unfortunate fish, I dare to look across.

The horse paces, stomping and phasing in and out of the shadows. No sign of the wolf. Maybe the river washed it away. I blindly search for sticks or branches, my hands scraping over the riverbank as I try to keep the nightmare in view. It's starting to edge closer to the running water.

Two small sticks sweep into my hand and I wedge them both at an angle in the soft bank. It's small, but it makes the nightmare nervous. Any sort of crossed item, or crossroads, or moving water—it confuses them, distracts them from the simple path toward whatever prey they've been sicced on. And gives me the courage to look a little harder in the darkness to find more. I'm able to find a bigger set of sticks and make another X. The nightmare backs up.

Two logs make a crooked X. Enough for the nightmare to trot backwards, snorting in fear this time. I don't look back as I push my tired legs into a shambling run, heading downhill, without much thought beyond get away, find a path from the mountains, and get help.

17

REMY

The low rustle of the night-filled mountains surrounds us as we pick our way up a slope, across a wide meadow, tracing ever upward as we go. I'm in the lead, following the tracking spell still spinning in the back of my head, sometimes calling it up to lie in a twisting, shimmering blue line up the mountain to make sure I'm not leading us astray.

No light except for the moon and stars. We're far enough out from the city to avoid the light pollution, and the gentle rustle of leaves and distant bugle of elk is a little eerie in the piecemeal darkness.

The grif squad stayed at the drop-off point, waiting for Besim to contact them on the long-range radio if we need backup.

We trek for an hour, footsteps falling lightly, and a few muffled curses when boots slip or sink into soft dirt and leaves without warning. Quiet falls abruptly and I whisper a soft halt seconds before the clatter of something coming at us sounds. I flit ahead, pressing against a broad trunk. One glance back and the others have vanished.

A tap through the comms is the only thing telling me they're still out there. Whatever is coming is not small, and is very out of breath. A human noise breaks, and it's close to a sob. I wait until it passes, then step out. Besim mimics, looming as a sudden wall and the figure halts but my hand is over its mouth before it can make a sound.

Cieran and Dejan appear as the figure goes limp in my hold.

Cieran jolts in surprise. "Agent Alder?"

Dejan lifts a hand covered in gentle light and I release the agent. She recoils a little from the light, turning to show red-rimmed eyes in a dirty face. A surprised "oof!" breaks from me as she rams against me, her arms squeezing around my rib cage.

"I'm so sorry! I couldn't stop them from taking him. She has him, and I…"

My arms slowly fold around her, and her words trail off into shuddering breaths. I really hope she's not about to cry. Her hold tightens and I wince. I shift to peel her away, demand where Blair is, but she flinches and I feel the stickiness of blood.

Dejan sees it too and lifts his hand higher.

"Are you okay, Agent? What happened to you?" I touch her upper arms instead, and she wobbles a step back.

"Got kidnapped…dragged from a lair by nightmares…" She scrubs a hand across her eyes, smearing dirt and tears. "Chased through the woods. Is this standard weeknight stuff for you guys?"

I want to know about Bear, but she's still shaking. "Are you okay?" I gently ask again.

"I…I think so." She looks around, taking in the sight of us again. "You g-got here fast."

I'm itching for answers, but Cieran's faint head tilt holds it in for now. Dejan gives a slight nod. She's clear. No tracking spell or glamour disguising her as something or someone else. Something I should have done, should have been on top of. They're already covering for me, and I need to get my head on straight because they can't cover forever.

"Sit for a second, Agent." Dej touches her wrist and guides her over to a fallen tree.

"Okay." She's hovering dangerously close to outright shock. Blood and dirt stain her shirt, ragged holes torn in the shoulder and the bottom half. Her jeans don't look much better. Dejan slings off his pack. She gulps some water from Cieran's canteen.

Dejan flicks his fingers and the light pops into a small bobbing circle. He pulls out his med kit next and dons gloves. "Let's see what we got here."

I've only ever really seen him patch us or other soldiers up, and it's usually done with his same abrupt manner. But maybe the elf does have a bedside manner, because his voice is gentle and he waits for Alder to hand the canteen back and shift to let him come closer.

Cieran's fingers drum the canteen as he waits for Dejan to assess.

"Anyone happen to have an extra shirt?" Dej asks. "I'm going to have to cut some of this."

Alder starts to flush, but we're already taking mental stock of gear. We left in a hurry, mostly just tossing extra canteens and whatever ration packs we had left over from last mission into bags. We didn't pack out for a lengthy mission.

But. "I think I do."

I dump my pack and start to rummage. Dejan slices through the shoulder of her shirt, and she keeps it tucked up enough to cover as he starts to treat her shoulder. Blunted teeth marks are visible under smeared blood.

Besim slides off to establish a perimeter. Cieran helps tear open gauze packs, and I try to keep patient. Though every look at her face holding a hollow-eyed shock, and the injuries clearly sustained escaping Maeve, keeps me from exploding.

Her breaths come a little less shaky by the time Dejan finishes and sets the last bloody gauze into the pile at his feet. She limps over as Cieran and Dejan start clearing the remnants.

I offer the thermal I've been bunching in my hands. "It's going to be big and I've no idea how long it's been in my bag, so sorry if it's got pack smell."

A faint smile spears across her face and she takes it. "As long as it's got the right amount of holes, I don't really care."

My lips twitch for a second. "Don't go too far past the light. Besim is out there somewhere, but we'll turn around."

She goes red again, but nods and slides past me. Back in seconds, ruined shirt in hands. Mine is definitely a few sizes too big and she's tucked it into her jeans which have a few rips and plenty of dirt and blood too. She's going to be out of luck with a replacement for those. I take her shirt and fold it up into my bag. Leave no trace.

A soft clearing of her throat draws my attention up. She stands beside me, darting a glance over at Dejan and Cieran still clearing signs of us away. I slowly rise, pulling my pack back on. She's rolled up the sleeves and clenches her hands together.

"Um..." Her voice barely rises above a whisper. "We can agree Ballagh is the worst already, but she said something...and I just..." She looks at me and my face is the one heating. I focus on her hands instead of her flushed cheeks framed in tangled hair. "I think I can guess why you had a completely different reaction than the other guys on that list. Fates, I'm so sorry, Remy."

Her hand reaches out halfway, then draws back. I sort of want to vanish into the woods.

"And I'm sorry if I crossed a boundary by hugging you a minute ago. I've just never been so glad to see someone before."

"It's okay..." I halfway look at her face.

"She's twisted up inside and really powerful, and if...if anything happened, then it wouldn't have been your fault."

I still don't know if it's shame or relief, hearing those words.

"And I'm overstepping again, and you don't want to talk about this..." Her hand presses against her forehead.

"No, it's..." My hand twitches between us. "It's something I...hearing that is...I just..." I don't know what I'm trying to say around the tangled feelings and heat in my face. "Thanks for saying that."

That part is true and, as her hand finds mine and squeezes gently, the heat drains from me, replaced by...calm.

"And I'm really sorry I couldn't keep her from taking Blair." Tears bud in her eyes, and now I'm the one squeezing her hand.

"You said lair. You know where they are?" I ask. Cieran is at our side in two steps.

She gulps a breath, mastering the watery glint in her eyes. "Well, I'm not sure which direction I came from. Or how we got there. Or..."

Cieran holds up a hand. "Deep breath, Alder."

She obeys and starts telling us what she knows. Maeve is somewhere up mountain, in a hideout filled with nightmares, maybe a physical crony or two, and Blair. From the amount of noise Alder was making before I grabbed her, I'm sure we can follow her trail back up mountain no problem.

"If it's any consolation, I really don't think she'll hurt him." Her green eyes find me again. "She really only seemed interested in…you." It's said with some apology, and I cross my arms as if to hide from the feeling the comment stirs. Relief that Bear is probably okay besides being used as bait, and the same nausea amplified times ten with the threat of seeing Maeve face-to-face again.

"Agent, a grif squad is farther down mountain," Cieran starts but Alder shakes her head.

"No, I'm going back up there with you."

We all look at her, brows raised. There's a different set to her jaw, something determined and almost fierce, that definitely wasn't there earlier today.

"If anything, you'll need someone to take care of Blair while the four of you do the 'stab and take down villains' thing."

A smirk twitches Cieran's mouth. "Fair enough. But you sure you're up for this?"

"I'll even try not to slow you guys down." A bit of life springs back to her features, and a faint bit of humor stirs in my chest. "And I'm assuming none of you have a hair tie handy?" She sinks fingers in the tangles, wincing.

"Actually, I do." Cieran unzips a small pocket in his armored vest.

Alder pauses. "Really?"

He extends a hair tie. "Yeah, my girlfriend lost one a few months ago and I've started carrying some around just in case, since Athina ticked off is a little scary."

"Disgusting, isn't it?" Dejan remarks, and Besim's chuckle gives him away in the darkness. Cieran's reply is modified only by the presence of the agent tying back a mess of hair.

"It's cute. Wait...the dragonwalker is your girlfriend?" Her voice rises a notch or two, but Cieran's got a dorky grin in place.

At least until I cut in. "I think the correct term is 'mate.'"

He shoves my shoulder so hard I take a step back, and my snicker joins Dejan's. Besim appears, his own smirk in place. Alder isn't sure what she's in the middle of, but she still smiles.

"All right, let's get going." Cieran waves me to take point again, but not before I catch him wistfully spinning the copper inlaid bond damp-ener around his wrist. He's always a little grumpy when she's got hers on, and from the little I know about Athina, she's got to be the same way. Whenever she and her fleet get to the city in a few days, she's probably going to be pissed. Cieran unexpectedly going out on a mission was not on the agenda.

One more thing that's going to be my fault in this whole messy situ-ation.

I forge ahead, following the pretty clear path left by Alder. She keeps up with us, but we're all taking it a little slower. I can't help but look over my shoulder every now and then, checking on her. But Besim has her in his sights, steadying her if she stumbles, and Cieran checks just as often.

Cieran calls a halt after another half-hour trek. We stay standing, but Alder collapses onto the ground, scraping a shirt sleeve over her forehead. There's a bit more light in the eastern sky, and we've got to cover more ground before the sun is up.

Besim extends a ration bar to Alder and she reluctantly obeys Cieran's instructions for small sips from the canteen. Dejan claps my shoulder as he moves past, jostling my hold on my own canteen that I've been staring at instead of drinking.

His carbon fiber bow is strung and latched into place beside the quiver on his back. He crosses arms over his chest, staying close as we watch different directions through the trees.

A brief sound of disgust follows the crinkle of the ration bar being opened. "You guys live like this on missions?"

I can't quite make out Alder's face in the lighting, but her disdain is pretty clear through the mouthful of dubiously flavored and compressed protein. Light chuckles come from Cieran and Besim, mirrored in my smile. A faint snort is Dejan's reaction.

"We should be putting that on the recruiting posters," Cieran says. "Cool weapons, terrible food."

Alder laughs softly. "Accurate."

"But we have the benefit of Remy," Besim says and my attention jerks to him. "He can almost make ration packs taste good."

"Really?" Her interest falls to me and I'm sort of flailing between her and Besim. Another faint snicker comes from Dejan along with an elbow against my arm. I scowl back. He can see it perfectly fine through the darkness.

Cieran maybe takes some pity on me. "About done, Alder?"

"Are you guys not eating?" she asks.

"Protein bars? You kidding me? Those are awful."

There's another crinkle and from the way her head tilts, I can imagine the look before a huff of a laugh.

"I had three cups of coffee earlier. I'm good." Cieran takes her wrapper and sticks it in his pack.

She stands with a bit of a groan. "How are you even functioning?"

"Mostly caffeine and spite at this point." He shrugs back into his pack. She laughs, but the rest of us know how true it is.

"Rem, how's it looking?" Cieran jerks my gaze from where it some-how landed on Alder.

"Tracker's still spinning. We're headed in the right direction at least. Trail's pretty clear even if I didn't have the tracker."

"You're welcome." A bit of wry apology comes from Alder.

I check my watch readout. "We've gained about fifteen hundred feet elevation in the last few hours. Got to be getting close."

"Okay. You and Dej scout forward, make sure we're clear."

Dejan vanishes to my left and I take the other side of the path. It's five minutes' stealthy walk before I hear the rush of the river. A chuff sends me dropping into a crouch. The sky is getting lighter, and I catch the silhouette of a nightmare trotting along the edge of the river before recoiling from something.

I edge forward. A few crossed pieces of wood are leaning precariously, but that's only part of the nightmare's distress. A dark lump lies on the bank, half in and half out of the water. From here, it looks vaguely wolf-like.

My eyebrow raises. It's not moving. Apparently, you can drown a nightmare.

A low warbling call lifts my focus to Dejan masked by brush. His hands lift and he signs a question. I reply affirmative and ease back until I'm out of sight of the river. I tap the comm in my ear and wait for Cieran's murmured, "Go."

"Found the river. One nightmare's still active over here."

"Think we can go around?"

"Maybe. I'll see what I can do."

"You remember how far from the river the entrance was?" His voice comes through and the question confuses me before I realize he's keeping the channel open for me to hear Alder.

Her answer comes faint. "Not really. Sorry."

"I'll head across and up," I say.

"Dej, keep an eye on that nightmare," Cieran orders.

"Got it," is the elf's reply. I tap confirmation and aim my path further right of the pacing nightmare.

The river deepens its chuckle and gives me a few rocks to cross on. I stack a few small stones in a pile and continue. Stop every few feet to send out a check for traps.

Nothing as I keep on, and I'm not sure if I'm worried I'm walking right into her trap, or astounded at her brazenness for not leaving out any wards. The tracking spell gains some strength and I angle further up mountain, crossing a swath of destroyed foliage.

Taking the gamble, I keep just outside its path, and follow until I find a small clearing and a doorway notched into the side of the mountain. I sink down into more cover and tap the comm.

"Found it."

18

REMY

MY FINGERS CURL INTO the soil, and I send out another seeking spell, spreading my hand flat against the ground, coaxing the magic to spread out and unobtrusively make its way to the door and beyond. It doesn't run into any magic warding at the door, doesn't hit anything in the tunnels and it gives me a hazy map as it does. I get impressions of footsteps deeper in the mountain. More than one set, so there's more than Maeve and nightmares inside.

But nothing stirs from the door or in the surrounding forest as the light grows stronger and stronger. Though nightmares could be watching me from the shadows and I wouldn't know until it's too late. One tap alerts me seconds before Cieran sinks down beside me.

"Nothing in or out," I report in a bare whisper. "I got heat signatures from several potential combatants. Lots of tunnels."

He nods, features settling into seriousness. "Tracker still leading in?"

My chin dips, not betraying the roiling mess inside. "I'm going to have to drop it before we go." I don't know what we're headed into, and I need to ditch any extra spell to free up my magic.

"Okay." He twists slightly, and I keep focused ahead.

"Rem and I will go first, get the door open. Dej, I want you next. Besim, cover our six. Alder, you're hanging back in the entryway until we're all in. We'll do a…" He pauses and we can all read the loss there. He was about to give a tactic from his old team, but none of us would know what it meant. "Clear as we go, and shout out when you find Bear."

"Got it." Our affirmations murmur back.

His fist taps my shoulder. "Keep your head, Rem."

"Yeah." I try not to make it an empty promise. But I'm afraid I might be stretched too many ways between the crew and Blair when we get in.

"Let's go." He doesn't give me time to keep thinking on it, rising up and stepping forward. I'm right beside him, dropping the tracker and my only link to Bear. We make it across the clearing without any noticeable trigger.

The door is set a few feet into the rock, giving us some shelter for the seconds it takes me to test the handle, and send out one more test for counter-wards or traps if this door opens. Nothing, and a simple charm undoes the locks.

It edges open under my slight push, and Cieran signals. I free my basalt sword and step inside. Dejan is at my back, sword drawn for close quarters. An empty hallway stretches ahead. Evenly spaced lightbulbs hang from the ceiling and illuminate our path.

"All in." Besim's voice barely sounds. I glance back to see Alder pressed against the wall, a bit of paleness reflected on her face from the light bouncing in through the door.

"What do I do?" she asks.

"Stay put until we come back. You're only moving if something comes through that's not us. Then get to cover as fast as you can." Cieran's shield whirs out.

"Okay." But she looks more ready to throw up than keep still.

"Move." Cieran doesn't give her a chance to ask anything else.

I stride forward, boots barely scuffing the ground. Bare whispers of tread follow as I head for the more substantial light ahead. We hit a split. Pause, then Dejan turns off into the new hallway and the rest of us keep going.

A room opens up, and I halt for a second before stepping in. Empty.

We keep going. Besim heads down another hall. Cieran leaves next, sliding into another room to check as I keep down the hall.

No sign of anything yet, and it's starting to get concerning. Taps and muted "clears" echo through the comm. I'd start panicking that she'd taken Blair and left if the tracker hadn't led right in. Another door appears to my left, and I ease forward. It's locked, but one touch with a quick muttered word unlatches it.

I crack it open, peeking in, and my heart stalls. I shove it aside and stride in, barely managing a quieting spell to keep Blair's yell from echoing out. He lunges from the small cot in the corner and I hit my knees, scooping him up.

"I got you, Bear. I got you." My heart throws itself painfully against my chest, relief tangling once again with anger. It's making my magic flare bright as I tightly hold him.

He sobs, trying to wrap himself around me entirely. "I want to go home."

"I know." I peel him away, brushing away tears from his cheeks and dirt from his pajamas, checking him over, making sure she hasn't done anything. Making sure it's really him and not some sadistic copy meant to distract me. "You hurt? Anything happen?"

He shakes his head. "It's scary here, I want to l-leave."

"We're going. I promise. I need you to be really quiet, okay?"

Another sob hitches, but he nods, reaching back to me. I pick him up, dropping the silencing spell as I do.

"I got him," I report through comms.

"Hello, Rem." Maeve stands in the doorway. Blair whimpers and my heart drops.

"This is easier, isn't it? No agents, no police. Just had to wait for you to show up." Her smile is sharp, predatory.

A shriek echoes from somewhere. Curses crack through the comms.

Maeve smiles. "Your friends found the welcoming committee."

"Rem, get out!" Besim grunts and a clash comes through before the comm goes silent.

I hold a reverse grip on the basalt sword as I raise it, fire spreading from my right hand and licking down the blade, feeding from the stone inlay.

Maeve tuts. "I didn't hurt him. Doesn't that get me a point and a chance to convince you?"

"No," I growl.

She steps forward, boots clicking on the stone floor. I want to give ground, but I don't.

"Come on. I need a kid with specific modifications and the easiest way to get that is doing the work myself. He's the closest I've gotten, which is why I need you again."

As if I didn't need another reason to be absolutely repulsed. "What did you do to him?"

She tosses her head, a bit of a scoff there. "Made sure I was going to get a healthy kid, Rem. Sure, he's a little different, but you should be grateful. I even made sure he looked like you to make it easier to take care of him."

A faintly sorrowful look creases her angular face, but I'm not falling for it. She's not sorry for what she did at all.

I shake my head, hating that I ever fell for someone like her. "No. You didn't want to see any part of you looking back when you kill him by throwing magic through him."

Maeve sneers, and a dangerous light glints in her eyes. "That agent said you'd figured it out. Always too smart, Rem. Come on, help me out again, then I'll set you up with whatever or whoever you want, and you can live happily ever after with all the money and magic you could possibly need."

My arm is tight around Blair, but he's not complaining, squeezing back with all his strength. Heat is building higher and higher around me, but he doesn't flinch. Sounds of combat are growing, and I hear weapons clash.

I take a short breath and cue up another *silence* charm with the hand holding him and tap his back, anchoring the spell there. I don't want him hearing or seeing anything that'll scare him more on the way out.

"I even double-checked the others just to make sure since I knew you'd put up a fuss about it."

Yeah, I'm being so unreasonable. I shift my feet into a more ready stance.

She rolls her eyes. "He can go free and so can your friends. As long as you stay here. It won't be that bad. I'll promise not to drug you again. We can do it however you want." She tries to sidle closer again, fluttering eyelashes like I'm going to climb into a bed right then and there.

The flame grows hotter. "Hang on, Bear."

I twist the sword, flinging scorching heat at her. She yells and throws up a shield barely in time. I keep up the flame, striding forward, pushing her back until the door is clear. I cut off the attack and stomp my foot down in a percussive strike, flickers of bright blue streaking out to slam into her.

She tumbles into the nearest wall, and I sprint back the way I came.

"Remy!" Her infuriated shout only adds speed. I skid around a corner, trying to twist and take the brunt of the wall on my shoulder and not on Blair. Cieran's shout echoes somewhere and I hesitate for just one second.

Shit. I keep going, finding the hallway outside and running to the entrance.

Alder lurches forward. "What's happening? I didn't know if I should go or not."

I detach Blair, deflecting each grab back for me even though it tears my heart. I end the silencing spell. "Bear, I need you to go with Agent Alder, okay?"

She takes him in her arms, but he still struggles.

"Bear." I press a hand to his cheek. His wide eyes fill with a little betrayal. "Go with Sara, okay. I'll come find you after I help the others."

"No, I wanna stay with you." Tears roll down his cheeks.

I kiss his forehead. "I'll find you as soon as I can. I promise."

He gets arms around my neck again and I can feel my heart splitting as I pry myself free. "Sara, get out of here and get down mountain. Find a place to hide."

"What about you?" she asks.

I undo a knife from my belt and push it into her hands. "Take this."

"Remy!" She's got Bear situated in her arms.

I dig into a vest pocket and pull out a coin. "Tracker coin. It'll lead us right to you."

"But..."

My hand rests on her shoulder, stilling her words. I've not trusted anyone outside my team for a long time, but right now I do. "Please. Get out of here. Look after him until I get back."

Resolve tightens her face. "I will. You be safe, and come find us."

I manage to smile. "I will."

One more kiss against the side of Bear's head before Sara heads outside. I wait long enough to make sure they're into the tree line before making my way back into the mountain.

19

Remy

Red eyes flare in front of me, fear rolling off the nightmare in waves. But I'm past caring. Nightmares aren't as powerful as they used to be before the Courts were broken, and iron or bright light can take care of them. We all have a piece of iron built into the tang of our swords, and all I need to do is pull the sword on my left hip.

But I don't.

Instead, I summon my brightest flame and it sears down the basalt blade, sending the rock inlay glowing and flaming as red as the magma it once was, and stab.

The nightmare shrieks and writhes as the wild magic flame makes its constantly phasing body solidify, then disintegrate.

It takes a moment of hands shaking and breath rasping before I get my anger under control. A warlock—especially a fire-based warlock—angry, is never a good thing and magic can easily spiral out of control. My son is safe, but my team is still here.

I pull my other sword free with my left hand, using a reverse grip. It's barely longer than the basalt blade, making the unusual drawing technique work. I keep it reversed as I start down the hallway again, pressed close to the wall.

The mountain has gone quiet. I halt, calling up another seeking spell, using the basalt to channel it better as I gently touch the sword tip to the ground. Heat from other living beings meets mine, and one is just around the corner ahead.

I creep forward, not even pausing as I spin around the corner, sword raised. It slams into something solid, and a knife is poised at my throat.

"Bes," I say.

Besim lowers his knife and moves his bracer-covered arm from where it had caught my sword.

"Bear okay?" He's breathing hard. Two nightmares slowly fade out in the hall behind him, and a real body sprawls nearby, unmoving. It's facedown and in street clothes.

"Sara's got him and she's headed away from here. Sarge and Dej?"

His silver stoneskin recedes as he reaches down to his leg. Slashes are torn through his trousers at the knee, but there's no blood. Six months ago, his stoneskin stopped working. And from the way he gingerly touches the area and gives a choppy breath of relief that it protected him again, he's still working through the trauma in some way.

"Haven't seen them yet. My comm's busted." A limp wire bumps against his armored vest, missing the earpiece entirely.

"Look who's ruining tech this time." I smirk, my eyes scanning each direction.

He snorts and picks up his longsword. "Yeah, okay." He taps my shoulder and we move out, clearing hallways as we go.

"Check in," I murmur through my comm and get nothing back. Besim softly mutters behind me and I'm pretty sure I can make that time number six he's cursed around me.

A growl warns us before nightmares attack. Two hulking shapes in minotaur form. Guess the wolves and horses weren't doing it.

These two are faster and dodge around hacks and slashes as we set back-to-back. Besim grunts and something pummels the back of my knees, twisting me off-balance as the nightmare in front of me charges. The bull head lowers and the horns slam my chest, foiled by the armored vest and chain mail, but still slamming me into the wall.

Screw this. "Besim, down!" I summon the same bright fire again. The nightmare recoils, freeing me from the wall and trying to run. Not before I slice through it, spinning to my left to catch the other nightmare poised above Besim's crouching form.

"You good?" I ask, and he levers himself back up.

"Yeah."

"Sorry." He's still been jumpy about wildfire since he got injured by a blast months ago and I just filled this hallway with it.

But his fist knocks against my left arm. "Don't be. Let's keep going."

We're five steps down the hall when a muffled, "Rem?" guides us to a smaller alcove. I summon a small orb of light to cast a bluish tint across Dejan. He sits against the wall, hands clamped around his bleeding leg, jaw clenched tight.

"Finally," he grits out. A knife is lodged in his thigh and his hands are white-knuckled where they clamp around his leg above it.

Besim pivots to keep watch while I crouch next to the elf. There's a body nearby and from the finely pointed ears and sharp cheekbones, I'm guessing some fae buddy of Maeve's.

"Hex," Dejan strains, sweat dripping down his face as the blade moves incrementally up his leg. I hate hex blades. Get stabbed and every time you move, they'll inch closer to your heart. Take one out with the hex still active, and it'll jump right back into you.

"Hang tight," I say pointlessly and a strangled sound comes from his chest. Elf magic isn't strong enough to do multiple things at once, like cast a holding spell on his leg to keep it from moving while breaking a hex.

Shimmering blue coats my hand and I carefully take hold of the hilt. My magic layers the knife, containing the hex, and I close my eyes, searching for the origin. It's usually keyed into some notch on the hilt, whirring around like a machine cog. All it takes is sliding a bit of magic between the gears and...the hex spasms and releases.

A strangled gasp comes from Dejan. He felt it. I release the holding spell on his leg and green magic flares up around his hands. I still have hold of the hilt and press my other hand to his chest, bracing him as he nods, and yank the knife free.

He curses loudly and liberally as it comes out and then the sharp scent of his magic takes over. It reminds me of chill mountain air hitting pine, a fresh tang that signals life. He leans forward and I grab the med kit from under his pack, opening it up, and tearing open bandage packs.

Dejan takes the gauze sheets with shaking, bloodstained hands and packs them against the wound which bleeds a lot less now that he's mended the torn muscle and blood vessels enough to not bleed out. Something that deep will still need stitches and several passes of magic for full healing—neither of which we have the time nor safety for.

He curses a few more times before he gets enough packed in and around the wound and wraps a longer bandage around his leg and cinches it tight. Dej fumbles in the kit, pulling out a smaller bag. I unzip it and pull out one of the slender patches. He peels it off the paper backing and sticks it on his neck over the main artery. Charm patches hold pre-prepped healing spells to help a medic spread his magic out. He's not going to use much more of his until we're out of here.

I sweep his pack closed and shove it back into place. Besim trades places with me to help Dejan up, and the elf roundly expresses his frustration as his leg buckles under attempted weight once Besim has him upright.

"You're such a baby," the half-troll tells him.

"I will stab you," Dejan growls, still leaning on Besim and trying to manage some weight.

"Just let me help," Besim says. Dejan grumbles but obeys as we move out.

"I thought I heard an elf." Cieran materializes in front of us, shield up and sword at the ready.

"Sarge." I tip my chin, relief hitting at the sight of him, even if blood covers the side of his face.

"Bear out?" he asks.

I nod, sheathing my longer sword now that he's here, but keeping the basalt blade in hand.

"Let's get—" His eyes widen and his shield sweeps up as he charges forward, trying to get in front of Besim and Dejan. I spin, whipping the sword horizontally as I form a magic shield. Something bright impacts and throws me to a knee, but my barrier holds. I lift my head to see Cieran just in front of me, braced behind his shield and Besim curled around Dejan. But all of them are okay and safely behind the barrier.

"Get behind me," I yell, flinching as something electric fizzles across my shield, sneaking through and shocking my arm.

They obey and I risk a glance forward. Maeve stands a few feet away, hands glowing bright and readying another spell to throw at me. A feral smile spreads when she sees she has my attention.

"Don't be like this, Remy," she hums.

I climb to my feet, settling my boots wider into a firmer stance, and the barrier strengthens. Scuffing announces the others backing up, and then Dejan barks a warning. Cieran whips around, crossing blades with another fae who's come up behind. A nightmare shrieks and Besim charges it.

Three more nightmares circle Maeve, hooves and talons scraping and smashing against the rocky floor. She smirks again, rubbing her hands together. The air crackles with her impending cast.

My knees bend, the action further centering me. I'm going to need strength and control to counter this. And perfect timing.

Her arms raise. My fire flares in response and my right foot stomps down. Anchor. Left fist slams against my chest. Strength. Then right hand still holding a pulsing, glowing basalt blade crashes against the underside of my left forearm. Each motion comes with a sharp word in Hawaiian, and with the last shout my barrier curls forward, engulfing the lightning coming right at me.

She shouts something in ancient Gaelic, her power intensifying for a moment, but I've got it caught. And I stride forward two steps, stomping down on the third and hitting my chest again, this time with my right hand, which angles the basalt blade toward her.

My magic, coiled around her writhing spell, rushes toward her. Her hand slashes sideways and she sways, twisting, like a dancer. The roiling mess barely clips her but smashes into the wall, causing a small implosion. She dives out of the way and I throw up another smaller barrier against flying debris.

"Nice catch." Dejan's hand clamps on my shoulder.

"Thanks. Doing okay?" I ask, barely sparing him a glance and waiting for her to re-emerge.

"Been better."

Besim appears and gets an arm around him. Dejan's features ease in relief. Cieran wipes his sword on his pants.

"Go." I step forward, keeping the shield up. Maeve moves sluggishly and the nightmares have vanished. Either dead or hightailed it to not get caught in that light. We move into the next hall, Cieran taking lead and Besim supporting Dejan right after.

I back up, making it two steps before something snags my foot. My leg spasms and I collapse, shield dropping. A strangled cry escapes as the muscles twist around each other, convulsing hard enough to threaten bone.

"Don't make me do it," Maeve warns, striding forward, arm outstretched and tugging on the spell she caught me in. I grit my teeth, raw wildfire pooling in my left palm before I slam it into the ground. It erupts, fed by my pain, and latches on to the stone to reach hungrily for her. She has to drop her spell, and I almost throw up at the sudden relief that's the pain disappearing.

Cieran grabs the strap of my vest and hauls me up. Cold rushes through and we're both gasping for air as the flame dies in the absence of oxygen. My magic panics, sending me reeling against the wall, trying to re-center as her counter-spell sucks greedily at my fire. I clench my fist and manage the release command, and my spell dies. I have milliseconds to get another shield up.

A keening sound announces I'm too late. But Cieran is already moving, getting his buckler up and taking the brunt of her returning shot on the surface. His shield has some warding runes and basic counter-spells etched on the surface. The dwarf designers should be really proud of how it holds against the heat building around us.

But he can't hold forever. I already smell smoke coming from the shield and it's starting to glow at the edges.

"Sarge." I get his attention, and grim focus furrows around his eyes. "Duck."

He hesitates only a moment before obeying. I throw my arm over his back, hand open wide and protectively coated in wildfire into the path of the firebolt she pushes at us. Cieran spins from under me and he's at my shoulder, ready as I try to sink fingers into the oncoming fire bursting against my hand.

"Remy!" she shouts over the roar of the flames.

I slam the flat of the basalt blade against my raised forearm, bolstering my counter.

"You and I can do this all day, right? But your friends can't."

Cieran curses and I refuse to turn at the sounds of combat erupting behind me.

The blast abruptly stops but I don't change my position except to widen my feet a little more. Center. My sword hums with contained power, both hers and mine that got caught in the basalt. It's fighting there now, the magma dragon gift trying to dominate her invasive magic.

"Come on." She tosses her arms. "I'll call off the dogs. Just work with me here, and your team and the kid can go home safely. Promise."

For a brief moment I hesitate, sword lowering. They can get out, find Bear and Alder, and get clear of the crossfire of me and my mistakes. She sidles closer, sensing it.

Silver flashes and she jerks a hand up, magic coiling around a knife about to impale her chest.

"Try again, *crytch*," Dejan snarls behind me.

It shakes me free, and I slam the sword hilt against the wall, releasing all the pent-up magic into the stone. It implodes around us. Her rage is drowned out in the clatter and I scramble back, barely dodging, but catching my foot and falling.

I'm dragged free by the strap of my vest again and Dejan sprawls awkwardly beside me.

"You *firren* stupid?" He shakes me, shouting in my face. I don't have an answer and it's partially because of the fear in his eyes. Fear that I might have really given myself up.

Besim hauls me up. Sweat trickles down my cheek and tremors have started to ripple through my forearms. My magic is starting to deplete. I'm going to need a break from casting soon. Cieran gets Dejan, the elf listing over his wounded leg. Rumbles come from down the hall, rocks shifting as she tries to clear the way.

Dejan grabs my arm, staggering as he does. "Don't you *firren* dare."

I grip his shoulder, jerking a nod. She's almost through and as I turn to face her again, two other shapes, more substantial than nightmares, flank her. I've got to stop her long enough to get out of this maze.

"I'm going to collapse it," I tell them.

"Then let's hustle," Cieran says.

I sheathe my basalt blade, grabbing a few palm-sized bits of debris from in front of me. I can do this on the way out. I follow them down the hall, coating one rock in humming fire and slamming it against the wall. It sticks, and I move on, repeating the same action with the other four pieces.

Light shines ahead and Besim practically picks Dejan up to move faster toward it.

Maeve shouts my name one more time. "You think these are going to stop me?" She rounds the corner, holding one of the rocks.

I shrug and slam my palms together. Her eyes widen and she drops it as each latent spell activates and explodes.

I run, stumbling after the others as the mountain shakes, groaning all the way to its bones. Cracks race ahead of me in the ceiling, the floor, the walls. I should have thought this through.

The entrance gets closer and closer and the others break free, staggering across the clearing. Falling rock hits my shoulder, twisting me off course. I push against the wall and keep going. Then I'm free, dust and debris spitting me out of the tunnel. But the mountain's not done and the ground heaves beneath my feet, throwing me on my face. The ground opens up, a new trap coming for me.

The crew has to be tired of pulling me to my feet, but Besim does it again. My legs buckle and he half-drags me by my vest as I scramble along, trying to outpace the crack.

Until suddenly, it stops. The mountain quiets. And I'm sprawled on the ground, boots a mere inch from the rent earth.

For a moment, it's just ragged attempts to catch breath all around. Then Cieran's huffing, "*Shit,*" has a desperate laugh breaking from me.

My shoulder's jarred by Besim's hand, and Dejan picks himself up off the ground. I stare at the place the door used to be, the mountain now folded over itself to cover it up. I have no idea if she survived. Don't really care to stick around and find out.

Cieran kneels by me. His fist presses against my chest and he nods. My hand clamps over his wrist and I squeeze. He got us out of there just as much as I did.

"Come on," he says, and hauls me, once more, to my feet. "Let's go find Blair."

20

SARA

THIS MOUNTAIN IS ABOUT to get another intimate look at my face. I stagger and barely manage to keep upright, boots sliding on some fallen leaves. Blair wrapped around me is not really helping my balance, but I'm not letting him go.

"Hang on, kiddo." It's about all I have breath for as we keep going. It's just the sound of me tearing through the woods. They won't need the tracking coin in my pocket because I'm sure I'm doing an even better job of leaving a trail this time.

Thunder breaks out behind me, and the ground shudders. Blair whimpers and something similar catches in my throat. I keep going a few more feet, but no other sound comes. My side cramps, and I find a spot sheltered by rocks and trees for us to hide in.

I'm definitely not made for field agent. The required gym time every week definitely didn't get me in any shape for this. The mountain shakes again, a groaning sound tearing through it before rebounding against the other low peaks.

I tuck back as far as I can into the shelter of the dell, keeping Blair snug against my chest, drawing my knees up, and pressing hands over his head. The shaking stops, a few more ragged groans echoing from somewhere deep. I move my hands but Blair tucks tighter against me.

Minutes, hours, seconds? I'm not sure, but they creep by. Silence remains around us except for the tentative rustle of wildlife. I'm finally brave enough to nudge Blair.

"Doing okay, Blair?"

"Where's Dad?" he whispers back, head still pressed against my shoulder.

"He's coming. I know he is." The look on Remy's face as he said goodbye didn't really leave another option. I hope the rumble was something getting dropped on Ballagh and not on the team. I'm still holding Remy's knife in one hand, and I hope I can muster that burst of insane courage again if we're found by someone other than the team.

He sniffles and adjusts so his arms are pressed between us. "And then can we go home?"

"Definitely." I'm ready for a shower and a bed and something to help me forget these last twenty-four hours.

A whisper of a sound draws my gaze up, and my mouth opens to scream reflexively, but something stops me. Remy crouches with his hand outstretched, apology in the wince of his face. I understand and shut off the soundless cry. He lowers his hand and Blair whips around.

"Shh!" I get a hand over his mouth just in time. He makes a little growling sound and I release him to charge into Remy's arms. The specialist rocks back on his heels, eyes closing as he holds his son.

Cieran comes around, hat still on backwards, and covered in the same dust streaking Remy. As I struggle up to my feet, I see Dejan leaning on Besim, one leg pulled up awkwardly. They're all bloody and beat, but here. They smile softly at the sight of Remy and Blair, then I get nods, even from the elf.

"Doing okay, Agent?" Cieran asks.

"Yeah." Now they're here, I'm turning into a jittery mess. "Only slightly traumatized."

He chuckles. "I can work with that." The sergeant reaches down to touch Remy's shoulder. "We need to keep moving."

Remy nods, and then I'm locked in his intense stare. "Thank you." There's so much packed into the tremoring words, and all I can do is nod and blink back tears. He climbs to his feet, still holding his son.

Cieran presses a hand to the boy's head, getting a slight peek from him. "He okay?"

Remy nods. "She didn't do anything. She's a lot of things, but she wouldn't lie about it."

"Good. Rem, I need you back on point." Apology shines in Cieran's eyes. Remy seems to collapse a little bit, but then agrees. He looks to me again, and I reach out to take Blair.

"We already know I can run with a kid. I've got this."

He gives a faint smile, and Blair comes back over more willingly this time. Cieran slides around to help Dejan distribute his weight a little better. His dark grey trouser legs are stained, and a rough bandage wraps his thigh, but he's back to glaring so it must not be too bad.

Remy backs away a step, making sure I've still got his son, before leading the way forward.

21

REMY

I TRACK A PATH that'll get us downhill as fast as we can. I want to keep checking on Blair, but I need my focus forward and making sure our trail is covered with a spell sweeping along behind us. We keep a fairly steady pace for twenty minutes before Dejan barks a rough curse.

"Bleeding again."

I turn to see Besim and Cieran lowering him down to the ground. Dej's face is even more thunderous than usual and he jerks at his med kit. I don't know much elvish but he's definitely cursing every fae guard and nightmare we ran into. He declines help, and Cieran gives me a nod.

I make immediately for Alder, still standing somewhat awkwardly holding Blair. "I've got him for a minute."

She hands him over with a smile, shaking out her arms once they're empty. The way she rubs at her face has me leaning a little closer around the bundle in my arms.

"You okay?"

Her smile flashes again, this time showing her weariness. "Yeah. I finally have my proof for Fortin that field work is not for me."

My chuckle joins hers.

"I will be gluing myself to a chair if needed. Only data analysis for me." Her hand moves in a chopping motion.

"I don't know. You haven't been completely dead weight," I say.

Her nose crinkles a little when she smiles and I jerk my attention from the sight, not sure why I'm even looking.

"Oh, here." She holds out my knife she's still clutching in one hand.

"Keep it for now." I shake my head. "We're not home yet."

She falters slightly. "I was afraid you'd say that." But then it's a forceful straightening and brightening of features. "Any idea how much longer we'll be out here?"

I check over my shoulder. Cieran's got his map out and is checking sun position. I might be able to track almost anything, but he's one of the best navigators there is. His photographic memory comes in very helpful.

"Cir will know. I took us off the straight path back to the grif squad. But looks like Bes is calling them." The half-troll has the radio out and is talking, coordinating a landing zone off Cieran's map for the griffins. Hopefully close.

Her lips thrum with a sigh. "Okay, I'm counting on all of you to help keep my trauma to a minimum here, so I'm going to go ask. But if I have to eat another of those bars, I'm officially billing you guys for my therapy."

I can't help my grin as she backs away and heads to Cieran. Blair shifts as I sink to the ground, settling him more in my lap.

"Dad?"

I look into his serious face. "Yeah, Bear."

"That lady...the scary one...she said she was my mom." His brow wrinkles. "But I don't have one."

I swallow hard, but there's no getting out of this one. This experience is not one he's going to forget. It still takes a moment for me to force the truth. "She is, Bear. But she's not a good person. She sometimes hurts people and doesn't feel bad about it."

"Like she doesn't say sorry?"

Good, he's offended by her behavior. "Yeah, doesn't say sorry. And moms...moms don't leave their kids with a dad and never come back."

He thinks on this, brow still furrowed, and hands tucked together in his lap. "Can I get a different mom?"

A faint sound comes from me. But instead of saying no outright, something in the last twenty-four hours has me saying, "Maybe some-day."

"Dad?"

"Yeah, Bear?"

His arms come around my neck and he presses a kiss to my cheek. "I'm glad you're my dad."

Well...I'm about to cry. Officially. I suck in a breath, casting a look up at the morning sky. "Me too."

He tucks up against me as I blink rapidly, gradually getting the rampage of emotion controlled. The chocolate I crammed on the way to find them is finally kicking in. My magic hums a little stronger in my veins as I snug arms around Blair, bringing a little bit of quiet along with it.

Dejan leans back against a tree, a silver-green glow around his fingers where he presses against his injury. There was a lot of blood, and he's got to be hurting even with his healing magic. Besim is on guard, keeping eyes out, radio tucked away. Cieran is on the opposite side of our little spot, attention split between Dejan, me, and the woods. He's spinning the bracelet around his wrist. We're not moving, so I'm assuming the grif squad is coming to us.

"Can I join you?" Alder's voice pulls my attention up. She smiles apologetically. "I'm a little nervous to go anywhere near him." She jerks a thumb at Dejan.

A small smile finds my face. "Have a seat."

She lowers down, crossing her legs and tucking her hands over her ankles. "He doing okay?"

My hand smooths over Bear's hair and he nestles as close as he can with the armored vest and knife strapped to the front. "For now. It might take a bit to work through once we get home."

If Blair isn't going to be waking up every five minutes, it's going to be me until I feel able to relax again. Which might be never.

A touch at my shoulder has me glancing in slight surprise where she leans into me. "You're a really good dad, you know that?"

It brings a different sort of heat to my face.

"I heard his question and I'm not really sure how I'd answer that." Her lip catches in her teeth with a pensive stare across the clearing.

I clear my throat, wanting to deflect. "Two days ago, he was asking me why hermit crabs decided to live in the ocean, so..." I lift a shoulder and she grins. "Some questions are easier than others."

"So why did they?"

It's been a really long time since I've smiled back at a woman with a teasing expression and glint in her eyes. But I don't need wards to see the pure honesty filling her.

"A crab fell in love with a mermaid and jumped into the ocean. Decided to never leave, so he found a house."

Her laugh is low and clear. "That's a really good answer."

"He might be disappointed later." I adjust so the basalt sword's sheath isn't digging so deep into my lower back.

"Or he might have a really great memory of his dad."

Bear moves and I check on him, but he just turns a faint smile up at me.

"I've always wanted kids." Alder's wistful comment has me looking back.

"I can recommend doing the whole 'get married first then have kids' thing." There's no bitterness snagging around the words, and I'm surprised at myself.

She half smiles. "I'd have to get out from behind my desk first for that. Besides, I don't really want to inflict my family on some poor soul. I'm definitely the underachiever."

"The last twenty-four hours might give you a few stories for holidays," I say.

Alder rolls her eyes a little. "Well, I can't whip out magic like my elf half-brother." There's a shrug to cover up some hurt she can't really erase from around her eyes.

I lift my shoulder. "I'd rather have someone around who'll scrap with nightmares."

Red tints her cheeks. "Even if they feel like barfing all over your boots right after?"

I chuckle faintly. "Even if. But seriously." She seems to sit a little taller under my focus. "You didn't blink once. You're tougher than you think, and I'd take that over magic any day."

She looks at me, eyes glinting bright, before she gives a little nod, almost like she's proving it to herself. "Thanks."

I tip my head and check Besim and Cieran's positions. Dejan leans forward, tightening a bandage back around his leg. His jaw is set, and I'd offer but he's not going to accept my magic. I'd be casting blind anyway. I only know three basic healing spells for emergencies.

Blair starts squirming and then he's digging in the pocket of his pajamas. I shouldn't really be surprised when he pulls out a rock. I've found a beetle carcass in a pocket on laundry day before, so I definitely prefer random rocks.

But this one looks odd.

"Where'd you get that, Bear?"

The way he shifts it from hand to hand, frowning at it, has the unease rising higher. "The lady gave it to me. The scary one."

"Let me have it."

Alder sits straighter at the tightness of my voice. Bear's eyes are wide as he hands it over. I feel it as soon as it hits my palm. Heat and guiding magic.

"Cir!" I clench my hand around it, snuffing out the tracking spell before hurling it as far away as possible. "We need to move!"

His attention whips to me, and he misses the dark shape looming through the trees. Besim barks a warning and lunges, but it's already dropping on top of Cieran.

"Not so fast." Maeve's voice sends my blood boiling instantly. She limps across the clearing toward me. I shove Bear at Sara and scramble to my feet, raising a hand, but Maeve is quicker. A clap of thunder and I go flying, breath knocked from me as I skid across the ground.

"Rem!" Dejan is halfway up. Alder huddles over Bear on the ground, unsheathed knife in hand. His cries urge my limbs back to work and I scramble up.

A strangled scream stalls me. Cieran's on the ground, darkness swirling across his face, a gut-wrenching sound coming from him. Besim is trying to get to him, but fights off another nightmare.

"Look out!" Alder shouts.

I'm hurled to the ground, spine bending painfully around the sword scabbard. Blackness coils around my arms, tightening with every struggle.

"Change of plans, Remy." Fury covers Maeve's face. Her perfect glamour is ruined, hair hanging loose and clothes ripped and dirty from me dropping the ceiling. "I kill your friends, sell the kid, and make your life an everlasting hell."

I get an arm a precious inch off the ground before it's slammed back down. I call my magic but she snarls a word in High Fae and the darkness starts slithering through my chain mail shirt, driving my magic away. She's closer, bloody grin stretching wide.

"I've got at least another two hundred and fifty years. I've got plenty of time for you."

Another word and thorns latch into my skin. A sound locks in my throat and my boots scramble against the ground before something pins them. My skin peels and shrivels away from the thorns which dig deeper each time I try to call my magic. Noise breaks free and I can't hear her voice as her knee drives into my gut. She leans over me, a hand gleaming silver raised above my chest.

I panic.

I'm helpless. Just like last time.

A blur of grey and blond tackles her off me with a furious sound. Her scream is a mix of surprise and pain. I stare, still trying to tear free of her spell.

Dejan rolls past her, leaving an arrow in her side. He tries to get up, fury on his face. Pull his knife and finish the job.

She's faster, and her spell-coated hand hits his chest.

22

REMY

"DEJ!" BESIM'S DEEPER SHOUT joins mine.

He collapses, her hand pushing him into the ground. And he's not moving. Maeve leans over him, then another arrow hits her side and her back arches, a wordless cry cast at the sky before she crumples to the ground.

The bindings holding me vanish, and I dumbly trace the path of the arrow back to Alder, on her knees, trembling as she holds Dejan's bow, arrows spilled from his quiver around her. A body lies nearby, Dejan's sword sticking from it. Blair is a trembling ball behind her. I want to go to him, but...

"Dej..."

I peel myself up. A strangled sound comes from Cieran. Besim helps him up. His eyes are red and bits of black trail down his cheeks.

"No." He stumbles and trips over to Dejan, and his same terror at losing a crewmate propels me to Dejan's limp form.

I get there first, trying to find a pulse, shaking him, trying to get a response. I unstrap his tac vest and shove it aside, but there's no impact mark on the vest or his shirt to tell me what happened. Cieran crashes to his knees, blank horror in his eyes. Besim kneels at Dej's feet, ready to help with whatever we need, but I don't know what that is.

"Dad!" Blair sobs. I'm torn, but a quick glance reassures me that Sara's still got him covered, pulling him away from the dead.

"Come on, Dej." The words hiss between my teeth. I've finally got a pulse, but it's sluggish and *he's not moving.* I don't know what she's done. Foreign magic taints all around him.

"Shit." Cieran bows his head.

My hands curl against Dejan's chest. Stupid elf, getting himself hit with the spell meant for me. Everyone's been hit in the crossfire, wedging their way between me and Maeve like they can do anything to distance me from her and everything she's done.

I'm shaking and it's a tear-inducing mixture of rage and exhaustion and fear and shame. It all escapes into a shout and I slam the heel of my hand against his sternum, throwing a bolt of energy into him.

He jolts and his eyelids flicker. I repeat the action, doing the stupidest thing a warlock could do and just pouring raw magic into someone. But I'm not losing someone because of her. Not losing my brother. Not letting Cieran lose another crewmate. Not telling Blair why Uncle Dej isn't coming around anymore.

Once more and then a breath jolts though him and he convulses, wrenching upright and gasping for air. Cieran catches him and Dejan's wild gaze swings around.

"Rem..." His voice is hoarse. "That *firren* hurt."

My hands against the ground barely catch my relieved collapse. "You good?"

He leans on Cieran, rubbing his chest, a frown in place. "I don't know. I don't feel right."

Cieran nods. "Bes."

But Dejan tries to straighten, jabbing a finger at Besim. "Don't you dare try to pick me up."

Besim chuckles, but it's mostly relief. He claps Dejan on the shoulder.

Dejan's fist knocks my chest, resting there a second. "Go make sure Bear and your agent are okay."

I just nod numbly, staggering over, dropping to a knee in front of Alder, who's gone a definite green color.

"Oh Fates," she whispers, and then twists away from me and retches. I gingerly pull her ponytail out of the way as she officially vomits. Blair tackles my side, drawing a muffled curse from me as I discover tender shoulders and arms along with steady drip down my thermal.

Alder straightens, wiping sleeve over her mouth.

"I don't want that shirt back," I say. A sobbing laugh escapes her and then her forehead is leaning against my shoulder. I don't reach out to her, but my hand twitches like it might want to.

The rush of wings and treetops bending in sudden wind has me squinting up at the grif squad coming to land. Their massive lion and eagle bodies compress, golden wings folding back and vanishing, as their bulky human frames take their place.

Cieran gets to his feet with Besim's help. "Beck."

"Always something with you, Cir." The squad sergeant looks around the clearing.

Cieran smiles tightly. "Two wounded and two civilians to get back to the hospital. If one of your team can stay to guide another squad in, Besim and I will run cleanup out here."

I want to protest, offer to stay, but Alder still leans on me, Bear is latched on, and I can barely muster the strength to get up off the ground.

"You got it." The shifter starts giving some orders, and Cieran is beside me, extending a hand down.

"Get them back safe."

"I will."

Dejan is feeling well enough to curse at Besim as the half-troll practically carries him over to a griffin and helps him on. Alder shakily climbs on another and Cieran hands Blair up to me.

Blair tentatively runs a finger down a neck feather, eliciting a swiveled look from the griffin's eagle head. He draws back against me, but there's a friendly parting of the beak and a blink of a large golden eye.

"Hang on." I tuck arms around him, pressing low to the leathers as the griffin crouches, body tensing, and hindquarters springing off the ground.

My eyes are slipping closed, adrenaline fading and weakness tugging at my joints from the dampness sticking my shirt to my skin, when we finally land on the hospital roof.

23

SARA

I'VE NEVER BEEN SO glad to put my feet on solid ground. I'm not great with heights or hospitals, but I'd rather be stuck in a hospital than speeding through the air on a griffin ever again.

Nurses and doctors greet us on the rooftop landing pad. Based on the efficiency with which they move, they must do this pretty frequently. Dejan manages to slide down by himself, still looking grumpy. Once I get to the roof with a moderate amount of grace and a faint huff from the griffin who generously put up with me, I look for Remy and Blair.

Remy is still on the griffin, his arms wrapped around Blair. A nurse waits for him, but he's just sitting there, focus on something else entirely. I hurry over, some sense urging me to get to his side as fast as I can. The nurse glances at me, then focuses back on father and son.

"Remy?" I say cautiously.

He jolts and looks down at me, and I see the reason for the unfocused eyes. Red covers his hands and soaks through his chain mail. Blair is asleep, which is a good thing since seeing his dad bloody is not going to go well.

"Do you want me to take Blair while you get down?" I ask.

He gives a slight inhale and nods. Boots stomp over and Dejan stands next to me, hunched over and hand pressed to his chest, but focus entirely on Remy.

Pain creases Remy's face as he lowers Blair down. I rise on tiptoes to take him, Blair stirring more awake during the transfer. But he settles once he's curled against my shoulder. The nurse and Dejan steady Remy as his boots thud onto the roof next.

Another nurse reaches for Blair. A rush of movement announces Remy shoving between me and the oncoming medical professional.

"No."

I lean away from the gravelly threat in his voice, even though it's not directed at me. He's drawn a knife, though he's a little unsteady on his feet.

"He'll need to get checked out too," the nurse says soothingly, apparently not freaked out by a pissed off Drax soldier bleeding all over the place. "We'll take him down to pediatrics."

"He stays with me."

"Rem." Dejan staggers closer, and taps Remy's wrist.

"No one is taking him." Remy doesn't shift his glare from the nurse. Dejan would probably argue, but he's folding forward, heel of his hand digging into his chest. They both need a doctor, and someone needs to figure out what Dejan got hit with.

"Sir." The nurse tries again, and looks like he's ready to signal the security guard lingering near the entrance. This is not going to end well.

Guess I'm up.

"Hi, Agent Alder from the BMA." I step forward, making sure I haven't shifted my hold on Blair. "Given circumstances, it'll be best if the specialist and Blair here stay together. It's been a rough night."

The nurse gives me a suspicious once-over. "Frankly I don't see why the child needs to stay with him." He glances at Remy.

A sound very much like a growl escapes the specialist. "He's my son."

The nurse raises a skeptical eyebrow. This guy is going to get incinerated. The security guard edges closer. I feel for my badge, but come up empty on my belt. Great. It's lost somewhere in the woods.

"Look, I'll stay with them both if that would make getting treatment started easier. I'll give you my badge number and you can call the office to make sure everything is aboveboard."

The nurse's brow is still quirked and distrust fills his face, but thankfully there's another doctor coming over. This one is a dwarf in a white coat, stethoscope with a cheery elephant face on the end around her neck.

"I'm on call for pediatrics today. I'll go with you all downstairs. I can check him while the specialist here gets medical attention."

Remy sways a little, but thankfully agrees. As soon as he does, another nurse lunges forward to grab Dejan's arm as the corporal's knees start to buckle.

"Let's move," the doctor says, not losing the cheeriness to her voice, and the other nurses and doctors spring into action, shepherding us through the roof door into the hospital. I turn just long enough to call a thank you to the grif squad, and get a few raised wings in response.

Dejan staggers and his skin is taking on a waxy sheen. A wheeled stretcher meets us. He's bundled on and they sprint down a hallway labeled SURGERY.

Remy crowds me, his steps all over the place. I lean my shoulder into him, and it straightens him out slightly. I can't support him and carry

Blair for very long, so when the doctor points into a room, I try not to loudly exhale relief.

She has me take a seat on the bed, and my aching body just wants to curl up on it and sleep. Remy slumps down beside me, and thankfully a different nurse comes in. The elf looks like he's probably ex-Army, tattoos covering muscular arms. They must have sent him to deal with possibly explosive soldiers.

But Remy is losing focus again, and mechanically helps the nurse take off weapons, vest, and chain mail shirt. The scrape of wheels against floor have me looking to the dwarf, now perched on a rolling stool.

"Okay, let's see what we've got here."

Remy watches cautiously as I peel Blair away from me and turn him so the doctor can check him out. He stirs, eyes fluttering and face scrunching. Then he jolts, tears starting before he's fully awake.

"Dad!"

"I'm right here, Bear." Remy's blood-crusted hand presses against Blair's chest. "I got you."

The nurse taps his shoulder, and Remy scowls slightly, looking exactly like his son. "The doctor is going to check you over, okay? Just like last time we took you to the clinic when you were sick."

Blair looks trustingly back and settles into my arms, letting the doctor get a little closer. She starts asking Remy some questions about Blair's medical history. I'm trying not to blush because now Remy's got his shirt off and I feel like it's weird for me to be sitting next to a very muscular, very shirtless guy.

The elephant nose on the stethoscope has distracted Blair, and he's giggling softly as he messes with it.

"Can I get some information about what happened?" the doctor asks.

Remy and I exchange a glance. This is not going to be shared around, that much I do know.

"Kidnapping and rescue," I say. "To our knowledge, he wasn't hurt at all."

The dwarf nods, anger twisting her cheery face for a quick moment. "We've had a few kids come through that got rescued from trafficking rings recently. This related?"

I nod, wanting to hold Blair closer or let him crawl into his dad's arms and just see him safe. Something that's probably not polite in dwarvish escapes, and then she lifts a smile.

"Guess they picked the wrong kid to go after." She turns the smile at Remy. I'm halfway bracing for some retort from him, but he's slumped forward while the nurse dabs at his shoulders. The aura of calm the dwarf exudes is helping, because I'm ready to curl up and sleep peacefully. Remy gives a faint smile and nods.

"I don't see any traces of magic or glamour, and he seems to be in one piece." The doctor scoots back. "I am going to put in a referral for our child psych team to come see him before he leaves."

Remy braces, but she holds up a hand. "I'll talk to the doctor who'll be managing your case. You two will get the same discharge day."

"Thanks, Doc." There's relief and something closer to another smile.

The doctor nods. "Any other family we need to call?"

If she's fishing for mom, she's dead on a mountainside because I killed her. My stomach flips again at the memory and if I had anything left in my stomach, I'd be two seconds from vomiting again.

"My parents..." Remy trails off. "Shit, I think they were here last night...I don't..."

"I can call them," I offer. I need to keep busy right now. I should also find my boss, who's probably here too.

"I can't put that on you." Remy shakes his head.

"It's okay." I force a smile. "I can give them more details than the doctors can. And I need to go start some reports anyway."

The dwarf concedes to me, and leaves. Blair falls asleep as I maneuver him down onto the bed.

"You sure?" Remy looks up at me when I straighten. From here, I have a better look at the lacerations on his arms and shoulders. I wince for him.

"Yeah. You need to keep getting treated, and I need to be busy for a bit." I keep the words light, but there's some unfair understanding in his face, and my insides twist up in a confusing way like they did on the mountain when he said he'd take me over magic. "What's their number?"

He gives me the information to contact his parents, and I escape the room, but not quite leaving the feelings behind.

I borrow the hospital's phone and find his parents at home. They're understandably panicked when I introduce myself and I have to gently forestall millions of questions to give them the update.

From there, it's checking in with the office and promising reports. To the nurse's station where I get a room number to go visit Fortin who made it through surgery and leg already on the way to healing thanks to the elven doctors' magic.

And it's in her room where she's propped up and eating from a tray of something vaguely resembling food, that I learn just how terrible *I* look, with a borrowed oversized shirt, hair a tangled mess, and blood and dirt streaked all over.

It's almost a stranger looking back in the mirror when she sends me to go look at myself. I'm not normally one to care overmuch about appearance, but something about the haggard sight has me cringing, understanding the looks of slight horror and general avoidance of civilians in the halls, the caution from the nurses. And something else at the thought of Remy and the others seeing me like that.

But they hadn't batted an eye, and I might not have known how bad it was until someone straight up told me. That sort of reassures, the fact that soldiers I definitely respect hadn't cared.

Self-consciousness still fills me though, as I leave Fortin with her assurance that she's on the mend, get an update on Dejan, and head back into Remy's room. He's got a short-sleeved hospital shirt on now, and the nurse is cleaning up supplies. I wait until he leaves to awkwardly come stand in front of Remy.

"Your parents are on the way. Dejan is still with the doctors," I say, hands scrubbing at each other.

"They say anything?" he asks cautiously, glancing toward the door like he might be expecting Dejan to stomp in.

I shake my head. "Sorry."

He doesn't curse aloud, but it's all over his face as he fumbles with his boot laces, finally just shoving them off. "Thanks. You get checked out?"

"Yeah." I wave a hand. "I'll be fine."

His brow raises slightly and I'm fighting off another blush.

"How are you doing?" I turn it back to him.

A breath cuts from him and he shifts his shoulders. "I don't know what he gave me, but I'm feeling pretty good right now." It's slurred. The nurse gave him the good meds.

It draws a smile from me. "You should get some rest."

"You too, Alder."

It's weird, having someone be this concerned about me. I shrug it off with a mock-salute. "Yes, sir."

He rolls his eyes, and starts to move, nudging Blair over, and lying down on his side. My cheeks warm again as I help pull blankets up over them, practically tucking in a grown man. His arm settles over Blair, and his son snuggles closer in his sleep.

I smile softly, and something about the sight—father and son back together and the case on its way to being closed—brings a different sort of satisfaction than anything I've ever done as analyst. This time, I did feel like I made a difference in the end, was part of something, not just hiding behind the numbers and passing along information, never seeing what came of my contribution.

"You didn't blink once. You're tougher than you think."

Remy's words replay as I back out of the room. It means a lot coming from him, a man who routinely jumps into danger without flinching. And...I don't know...maybe Fortin is right after all, and field agent could be a good fit for me.

One thing's for sure. I'm going to make sure Maeve Ballagh's case is permanently closed, and no one will ever try something like her again. And then I'm getting on the case to close down the trafficking rings so no kid is ripped from their home like Bear and like the other kids freed in the recent busts.

If it means helping families and protecting kids, I'm all in.

24

REMY

SOMETHING BRUSHES MY LEFT arm and it's a little damp. There's a mix of chill and thermal energy radiating from close by. Bear.

I crack open an eye. Sure enough, he's on his knees beside me in a hospital bed. He's got a marker. And that marker is smearing all over my arm. More specifically, the geometric shapes and swirls making up the magma dragon tattoo.

"What are you doing, Bear?" My words come smothered through a yawn.

His grinning face shoves into mine, angling to look me straight in the eyes. "Coloring your dragon."

"Oh really?"

"Don't worry. There is no pink." And he returns to coloring.

"That's a relief." The wryness is lost on him, but I don't move. I'm not going to be able to tell him no for awhile.

I lift my head slightly to check the time. Late afternoon sunlight angles through the windows. I've slept most of the day. But he's in fresh clothes, which means we had visitors while I was out.

"How long have you been awake?" I ask.

"A long time." He caps a marker and picks up a blue one. "Gram and Gramps are here. They went to go get better food. I've had a lot of pudding." A pleased grin wrinkles around his eyes.

Great. Tons of sugar.

"Sara brought these markers for me."

I make a mental note to thank Alder so very much for that.

"Can we go home soon?"

"I don't know, Bear. I have to talk to the doctor first." Tenderness is making itself known in my shoulders and arms, and I try to move enough to relieve it and not disrupt Bear's artistry.

"Dad." He softly touches a bandage taped on my upper arm. "You have a lot of these."

"I got a little banged up, but I'll be okay." With the amount of inherent magic I have, my body's threshold for healing magic to be added is a lot lower than other humans. Which usually means more bandages and small amounts of healing magic spread over a longer time.

Seriousness clouds his face as he sinks back on heels to look me in the face again. "What happened was scary," he says slowly. "And I wish it won't happen again."

I cup my hand around his neck and pull him close. "She won't ever be able to hurt you again, okay. And I'll always come to find you, no matter what." I know I can be a better father in a lot of ways, but this is one of my truths.

"But what if you get hurt again?" He pulls back, but one little marker-streaked hand presses to my chest.

"Always, Bear." I tug him back and plant a kiss on his forehead. "Always."

It takes a second before I can release him. And I have to clear my throat when I do. "I think my other tattoos probably need some color, too, huh?"

His grin returns, and he graciously lets me choose the color to fill in the swirls of my warlock marks. There's some freestyling before he's done, but he's happy and I don't really care.

My parents return with questions I can vaguely answer after Dad presses his forehead to mine for a long moment and Mom cautiously hugs me around my bandages and her arm in a sling. She's okay and Dad gives a small nod and taps fingers against my warlock marks, silently giving a blessing to keep using my magic in the service.

Mom drops a kiss on Bear's forehead and one against mine before unpacking the hot sandwiches and rosemary-coated potato wedges they brought so we don't have to eat hospital food.

It's late when they leave, and Bear has fallen asleep against my chest, my arms tucked around him. There's not really room for two on this bed, but I'm going to make it work because he's not getting taken two floors down to Pediatrics.

There's a soft knock and Cieran steps in. He's limping, still covered in some blood and dust, weapons strapped on. Must have just gotten in.

"Hey." He leans on the bed railing. "How we doing?"

"He's got a clean bill," I return in the same low voice. "I'm okay."

Cieran smiles as he catches sight of Bear's handiwork on my arm. "Sure?" he asks.

I swallow hard. "Yeah."

His raised brow has me looking away for a second. He's unfairly observant sometimes. Could beat out Besim if he wanted.

"I..." But it's stuck. I don't know if I can ever admit that for the brief second when he disappeared, I wondered how much easier my life would be without Blair. It didn't last, and I'll never let him go, but that guilt is still there.

He crosses his arms. "You ever talked to anyone about what happened? Besides us?"

I shake my head. The only thing worse than baring my soul to my crew might be baring my soul to a stranger.

"From my experience, it helps," he says. "It can't change what happened, but it can help you carry it better."

"I don't know."

"Think about it." He taps my arm.

"You okay?" I turn it back to him. Some redness lingers around his eyes. He looks well past exhausted. A sigh cuts through him.

"Tired. Another squad is finishing cleanup of the hideout. We were able to get in there and find plenty of evidence linking her to different organizations. Bureau will be throwing a party with what we found."

"Good." I'm ready to see all traces of her and her activities wiped from the earth. "What did she do to you?"

He pauses, swallowing hard, but answers. "From what I could tell, some sort of distilled nightmare spell. Conjured up some of my worst memories."

"Cir, I'm so sorry. I..."

"Hey," he interrupts before I can thoroughly beat myself up about it. "I didn't see you casting that spell. So don't take the blame for anything she did. It's not your fault."

"But you and Dej...you were only there because of me."

"Where else would we be?" He shrugs, and those simple words hit me in the chest. His fist nudges my arm. "We'll be around tomorrow. I'm going to dig up some info on Dej."

I nod, because if I try to speak, there's a chance I might dislodge the lump that's taken up residence in my throat recently.

One more gentle tap and then he's gone. I free a hand from around Bear, flip the light off, and lower the head of the bed a little more with the controls. It takes time, but I finally fall asleep, Bear safe in my arms.

25

REMY

AGENT ALDER IS BACK in the morning. She gets there before my parents, thankfully in enough time to distract Blair who's tumbling and running all around the room. I might actually be ready to send him home with my parents if I'm staying here longer than today.

He bounds over to her, reaching for the hug. She scoops him up and gets a full Bear hug. And I can't help but watch the way her smile widens.

Alder sets him down and he careens back over to me. "Dad, can she come over again?"

She's in clean jeans, and a short-sleeve-button-down, some bandages on her arms, and hair loosely braided over her shoulder. Still some circles under her eyes, but she's smiling.

"Don't feel obligated," I say softly.

She shrugs. "He likes drawing and books. He's my kind of kid."

And that shifts something in me. "I owe you."

Alder shakes her head. "You'd probably just say it's part of the job, right?"

My lips flatten in reluctant agreement.

A faint grin crooks her lips. "I will take a couple dozen batches of those chocolate cookies however, and we'll call it even."

I chuckle. "I'll set you up for life, Alder."

That gets a little blush across her cheeks. "And I'll probably have to come over to get them, right?"

I can't remember the last time I've invited someone other than my squad over to the house. Can't remember the last time I've felt so comfortable around an almost stranger. And it's got me saying, "I think he'd really like it if you came around sometime. I think we'd both like it."

Her hands twist together for a second, and when she looks at me, it's a little shy. "I'd like it too."

Blair has been watching quietly, and as soon as the words leave her mouth he jumps on the bed, arms pumping. "When are you coming?"

She laughs and I arch an eyebrow as I try to fend off an overexcited four-year-old. "Sure you don't want to rethink that?"

Sara shakes her head, still laughing. It grows as she sees my arm. "Was that the markers I brought?"

Blair crashes into my lap, gladly taking credit for his artistry.

"Sorry," she mouths to me, but I just give a sort of resigned shrug. At least he didn't color the hospital walls. It takes a second to realize that she's looking at my tattoos, the markings I've kept covered for five years. But there's just focus as she listens to Blair describe in excruciating detail why he picked each color.

My parents arrive a few minutes later. Sara gets a hug from my mom, and a solemn handshake from Dad. And I get a surprised look when Blair announces that Sara will be coming over sometime soon.

She excuses herself in the hecticness my parents' arrival stirred. And if they notice me watching her leave, they don't say anything.

—————

The doctor gives me the all-clear by the afternoon. Maybe she can read my desperation to get out, or maybe it's Blair rebounding off the walls, but we're given paperwork and I'm practically ordered to come back every two days for checkups.

Cieran is in the hallway, a serious expression on his face as he talks in a low voice with doctors. Dejan doesn't have anyone listed as emergency contacts outside of us, doesn't really have friends, and definitely no family outside of us. He's got a paper that says his crew sergeant can get updates if needed. I leave Blair with my parents and make my way over. Dejan was asleep when I stopped by earlier, and it looks like some bad news is on the horizon.

Not even Athina leaning against the wall a few feet away changes Cieran's expression. Besim stands beside her, arms crossed, the same seriousness lining his frown. We bump fists and I nod reassurance that I'm still okay. He musters a smile and waves to Blair down the hall.

A small smile flits across Athina's face as she looks at Blair. She's in her fitted black fatigues and boots, dark hair tinged in copper wrapped in a braid around her head, and just missing the dragonfleet breastplate and harness. Like us, she's completely comfortable openly keeping knives on her belt. Of course, she can also turn into a fifty-foot red-scaled dragon at will, so she doesn't really need them.

"He is a cute child." She looks to me. "He's very much like you."

"You calling other guys cute when I'm standing right here?" Cieran breaks in. Athina rolls her eyes at him.

"Thanks," I say. She probably doesn't know how much that relieves me to hear after everything. She reaches out and touches my forearm. Her hand is warm through the long-sleeve my parents brought, and the gift of the magma dragon feels like it hums in a greeting to her dragon magic. A friendly call, and the reason I've been comfortable around her and her team since the beginning.

"Cieran told me what he's allowed to, I suppose." This earns Cieran a narrow-eyed look and he tosses a hand.

"I'm trying to follow orders, hot stuff."

I mime a faint gag at the affectionate nickname he's got for her. She just makes a face back that says he could probably have given more details. He actually probably gave too many, knowing him.

Athina focuses on me again. "I'm glad you and Blair are all right."

"Thanks."

"Some of the info found links to some criminals from the Kirnae Archipelago and African mainland. We'll be putting together a joint task force," Cieran says.

Athina looks grimly pleased by this. I won't mind having some dragon shifters on our side.

"How's Dej?" I ask.

Cieran crosses his arms, unfamiliar seriousness falling over him again. Athina mirrors it, and from the way his eyes dart to hers, something goes through their mind bond. Besim and I exchange a glance. In the six months since he's been our sergeant, Cieran's never been this somber, which means it's something bad.

"Doc says whatever hit him affected his heart. It's still beating fine and functioning like normal, it's just got some sort of film spreading over it. Tests are inconclusive right now. They're getting a hold of some of the best casters and surgeons to try to figure it out. Physically, it seems like nothing is wrong."

"That doesn't sound reassuring," Besim says.

"Yeah." Cieran frowns. "I'm not getting much more from them, but maybe they don't know either."

I spin away, one hand clenching in my hair. My mind is all too happy to replay the seconds where Maeve had me pinned, glowing hand raised, then Dejan tackling her off and getting hit instead.

It's my fault.

"Remy." Cieran and Besim cluster around me. They're going to tell me it's not my fault somehow, like my mistakes from years ago didn't catch up and pull all of them into this, didn't get my family hurt and my kid mentally scarred for life.

"They'll figure something out," Cieran says again. "They've got the best on it."

But it seems empty. I try to nod, pretend like I'm not torn up inside.

What if it's not enough? If Dejan dies because of me, I'll never forgive myself.

26

Dejan

The flat, uninteresting walls of the hospital room stare back at me. I think I should care that it's so boring in here. I've barely moved.

I should also care that my crew is talking about me in the hallway. They probably think they're far enough away that I can't hear them. But elven vision and hearing is twice that of the average human.

Cieran is giving them the news. No one knows what's wrong with me. I can already hear Remy start to beat himself up over it. Like it's his fault.

I should be more pissed off about that. Go out there, surprise them that I can hear everything, and then smack some sense into Remy.

But I'm not moving.

I should care.

I move my head slightly against the pillow. It's paper thin and that should annoy me too. I haven't gotten up unless a nurse or my own body has made me.

I should care. I should feel something. Anger, frustration, annoyance. Readiness to get out and hunt down the trafficking rings that are hurting innocent kids. Make sure Blair is really okay. Play the game of Go Fish I promised him.

But I don't. I don't feel anything at all.

THE SERIES CONTINUES...

Stoneheart

CORPORAL DEJAN KOSTIC HASN'T been the same elf since saving his crewmate's life and getting hit with a fae spell. He's losing emotion, feeling, time...But he's going to keep going as long as he can because he's not abandoning anyone ever again. His condition worsens at the wrong time in the middle of a mission to take down a trafficking ring shuffling kids with magic across the Allied States Wastelands, and his team and their dragonwalker allies barely make it out alive.

The only thing worse than that is making it to the safe camp and seeing the elf he used to have a heartbond with before he cut it out fifteen years ago...

Doctor Tara Novak didn't think it would be an issue to coordinate with the Drax Guard team delivering rescued kids to her medical camp on the Allied States-Mexico border. That's her job. What she didn't expect was to see Dejan Kostic again. Not after he had their heartbond removed in a back-alley deal and vanished from Detroit fifteen years ago.

She might never forgive him, even if he's changed for the better. But the traffickers aren't giving up on their cargo so easily. When they kidnap

Tara along with some of the kids, Dejan follows, trusting his team to find them. He can't abandon Tara again, even with the spell slowly killing him—or when his criminal past comes stalking through the door promising vengeance.

ACKNOWLEDGEMENTS

Each of the books in this series challenged me in some way. And I think this book did the most. Once I learned Remy's backstory in the way that only authors can by both abrupt realizations and tiny hints given by the character, I sort of locked up. It was heavy, it felt like it wasn't *right* for me to do. And then I realized...I wouldn't hesitate this much if this same story was told from a female point of view. The reason it's so uncomfortable is because society at large doesn't acknowledge men's mental health. Doesn't acknowledge that assault can and does happen to men as well. And then it clicked into place. That's the reason I was given the story and Remy – to talk about it and hopefully show others that they aren't alone.

Equally important to me was to show immediate support from the other men in his life, from his family, and from the other female characters. The way it should be when something like this happens to a man or woman.

So thanks to Mollie who gently challenged me when I initially thought I shouldn't write this backstory. Thanks to Jenni and Brigitte for being faithful beta readers and making sure I didn't set the entire series on fire a few times.

Thanks to my family who always inspires the rock-solid familial relationships in my books in some way.

Always a thankyou to God for giving me the gift of storytelling, and giving the firm push to keep going when the stories feel weighty and hard. Thanks for giving me the weighty and hard stories sometimes. I always pray I can tell them with honor.

And thanks to you, reader. Thanks for coming along on the journey with Crew Six so far. Sorry for the little cliffhanger at the end ;). Buckle in, because Stoneheart's going to be a wild ride!

More Books by C.M. Banschbach

The Drifter Duology

Laramie was born to ride the desert wilds. And she won't let anything stop her, even a fearsome warlord who wants her captive–or dead.

A genius mechanic–and a rare descendant of the once-magical Itan–Laramie drifts from dusty town to dusty town in search of the family that was taken from her.

But her rambling desert journey becomes a game of survival when Laramie crosses a ruthless warlord's territory. Taken prisoner by one of the warlord's biker gangs, she befriends a quiet, dangerous man named Gered. After surviving hellish circumstances Gered is tired of fighting for a better life.

Laramie will always fight. And she'll stop at nothing to win their freedom.

Enjoy this pulse-pounding motorcycle adventure in a post-apocalyptic western setting with found family and being brave in brutal circumstances. Complete series available!

The Spirits' Valley Duology

A man born for war. A bastard raised in contempt. Only together can they defend their tribe from slaughter.

Fierce-hearted Comran is the chief's son and the favored choice to be the next leader. Then his father chooses Comran's half-brother Etran for the role, straining the loyalties of the tribe and reinforcing the distance between the two men. When Comran is offered the role of battlewolf, he is ready to do his duty—but expects no friendship in return.

Steady Etran has long been shunned as the chief's bastard. Becoming the chief brings even more hostility, so he offers Comran the title of battlewolf to maintain tribal unity. But can he trust this reckless warrior as his general when Comran has never stood by his side?

As tensions mount within the tribe, a traitorous act leads to war. Comran and Etran must overcome their inner demons and fight for their brotherhood before the Greywolves fall to their worst enemies.

Read now!

———

Subscribe to C.M. Banschbach's newsletter for free short stories and book/publishing updates!

About C.M. Banschbach

C.M. Banschbach is a native Texan and would make an excellent hobbit if she wasn't so tall. She's an overall dork, pizza addict, and fangirl. When not writing fantasy stories packed full of adventure and snark, she works as a pediatric Physical Therapist where she happily embraces the fact that she never actually has to grow up.

She writes clean YA/MG fantasy-adventure as Claire M. Banschbach.

Facebook – @cmbanschbach

Instagram – @cmbanschbach

Website (books and merch)– https://clairembanschbach.com/

Newsletter (routine updates and access to exclusive short stories)– https://c-m-banschbach.kit.com/0134a85703